1475

THE VERMILION GATEWAY

by

BELINDA DELL

HARLEQUIN   BOOKS

TORONTO   WINNIPEG

First published in 1970 by Mills & Boon Limited,
17 - 19 Foley Street, London, England.

SBN 373-01475-9

© Belinda Dell 1970

Harlequin Canadian edition published March, 1971
Harlequin U.S. edition published June, 1971

*All the characters in this book have no existence outside the
imagination of the Author, and have no relation whatsoever to
anyone bearing the same name or names. They are not even
distantly inspired by any individual known or unknown to the
Author, and all the incidents are pure invention.*

Printed in Canada

1475

CHAPTER I

The Senmonka School of Flower Arranging (Principal, Dr Akio Tanaka) had its premises on the edge of Kyoto on a wooded hillside with a stream running like a silver ribbon by its edge. To reach the low, curved-roof buildings, it was necessary to go on foot across a little wooden bridge and under a ceremonial arch lacquered a red so brilliant that, even in the light from a narrow moon, it shone clear and bright.

' The Vermilion Gateway,' Valerie Shansgate murmured. She felt a moment of deep delight. Here it was at last, the symbol that Dr Tanaka had used when he invited her to study Ikebana at his school: ' To understand Ikebana properly it is necessary to step through the Vermilion Gateway and follow the Path of the Gods,' he had said.

He had explained that the gateway was the entrance to Shinto shrines, and the word Shinto meant ' The Path of the Gods ', so that in effect what he was saying meant that to understand this most Japanese of arts it was necessary to come to Japan. But it had seemed an impossible dream at that time. Dr Tanaka was lecturing on flower arranging in Manchester at a hall of the university; Valerie, taken to hear him by a friend, had been enthralled.

Her father owned a small chain of flower shops in the town, so that she was often called upon to do floral arrangements on contract for hotels and shops.

5

One of her arrangements had attracted the attention of a Japanese lady married to a textile designer and settled now in Manchester. And it was due to her introduction that the invitation to visit the Tanakas in Kyoto had followed.

A year's painful scraping and stinting had followed while Valerie saved the air fare. Dr Tanaka and his wife promised to take her as a guest in their home, but of course one needed extra personal spending money.

Valerie had stayed one night in Tokyo before travelling on to the Senmonka School in Kyoto. She had been the guest of Mrs Misumi, mother of her friend Shizue, in a delightful little wooden house almost too small even for Valerie's small-boned frame. But she had enjoyed it, for she had made the acquaintance of Michiko, Shizue's sister, a tiny doll-like girl with a fringe of black hair above sparkling black eyes. Although two years Valerie's senior, she had somehow struck Valerie as much younger; at twenty years old, Valerie felt much more mature, much less sheltered, than Michiko—although there were many similarities in their lives, for Michiko too worked in a shop, an expensive dress shop in Tokyo's Ginza district.

Beaming with delight, Michiko had said, ' I have exciting news! Because of your visit, and interest taken in it by Mr Aro, my employer, he permits to go and study also at Dr Tanaka's school.'

' Michiko! You're coming with me? How wonderful!'

Michiko nodded. 'But not for so long. Mr Aro cannot spare me for the two months of your stay, but I shall have three weeks. Mr Aro says artistic flower arrangement will look good for the shop.'

Michiko had to stay with her uncle in Kyoto; Valerie had just dropped her off there—or it would be more true to say that Kan Tanaka had dropped her off, because it was Kan's car in which the two girls had been driven to Kyoto.

Kan had come on the morning of that day to escort them to his father's school. Tall for a Japanese, and extremely handsome, he had made a great impression on Michiko—much to Valerie's delight. On the journey he had chatted in English, explaining that he was a student at Kyoto University and was looking forward very much to talking English with Valerie. But she couldn't help noticing, with secret amusement, that it was to Michiko that he addressed two-thirds of his remarks.

Ken parked the car now by the Vermilion Gateway and raced ahead calling to his parents that he had arrived. The door of the dwelling house slid open and out tumbled two maidservants who ran to fetch the luggage. Behind them came Dr and Mrs Tanaka.

It came as something of a shock to Valerie when she saw they were both wearing kimonos. Last time she saw them, they had both been in European dress, and somehow they now looked transformed: older, more dignified. But they were kindness itself, leading her indoors, taking her coat and her shoes—

7

for shoes, she had quickly learned, must never be worn indoors in Japan—and offering food and drink.

The interior of Dr Tanaka's house was a judicious mixture of Western and Oriental. The now familiar matting—*tatami*—covered the floor so that it was necessary to remove outdoor shoes; but there were comfortable chairs to sit on, and when she was shown to her room she was relieved to find a divan bed with a good spring mattress and down pillows, quite unlike the thin mattresses on which she had slept in Mrs Misumi's house.

As sleep closed over her, she remembered she had forgotten to ring Clark to tell him they had arrived safely. It would have to wait till tomorrow . . .

Clark Cummings had been a new acquaintance yesterday, made within a few hours of her arrival. The taxi in which she had asked to be driven to the Misumi home had got hopelessly lost, and, being unable to speak a word of Japanese, she had been in a quandary until this tall, rather ugly Westerner came to her aid.

Having shepherded her safely to her destination, he had stayed to act as interpreter with poor little Mrs Misumi, who spoke not a word of English, until Misumi arrived home from the boutique. He had then taken his leave after a great deal of polite bowing. But he reappeared later that evening.

'Thought you might like to go sightseeing,' he explained, and introduced the European friend he had brought with him.

It turned out to be a great blessing, because with-

8

out them as escorts it appeared Valerie and Michiko would not have been allowed out: ' It is not proper for Japanese girl to go out much at night,' Michiko explained. And as Mrs Misumi seemed to want to watch Westerns on television, dubbed into Japanese, it would have been a dreary evening.

But with the two men as guides, Valerie and Michiko had seen something of the night-life of Tokyo. They went to a Kabuki play because Valerie wanted to see something traditional and Clark's friend, Toby Bates, seconded the motion. Valerie had sensed that Clark wasn't too keen, but she and Toby had enjoyed it greatly. Toby, it proved, was nearly as new in Japan as Valerie.

' I'm here to learn the ropes from Clark,' he explained. ' He's the Sydney manager of Lustre Jewels, of London, Tokyo and Sydney. Quite a big noise, he is,' he added, grinning from his honey-coloured eyes with impish amusement.

' And are you a small noise?' Valerie inquired.

' As yet, I'm afraid so. I'm a lawyer, actually—newly qualified. I'm here to learn how to handle contracts for buying pearls, which is the chief reason we have an office in Tokyo. Clark swans about a lot, buying pearls at Toba Bay—he's been with the firm about ten years, you know, speaks Japanese really well.' He paused a moment, looking puzzled. ' And yet it seems to me he doesn't really approve of the Japanese environment. He hates Japanese food and finds Japanese rooms uncomfortable—of course, anyone as tall as that probably gets cramp in them!'

Valerie laughed, but recalled how bored Clark had seemed at the Kabuki play, that extraordinary mixture of splendid costumes, stylized speech, slow-motion gesture, and drama. She felt a little guilty at dragging him there, yet was surprised that anyone could fail to love this beautiful, romantic country, and all its traditions.

One thing she had to admit was not romantic, and that was the standard of Japanese driving. When he learned that she was to go to Kyoto in Kan Tanaka's car, Clark had looked quite alarmed. 'Ring me and let me know you've arrived safely,' he begged.

And she had meant to do so, because even if she had little in common with him he had been kind, and she owed him at least politeness. But it had slipped her mind.

She was wakened by the sound of a bell tolling. She sat up, perplexed, then recollection came back to her as she took in the contours of the room and its sparse furnishing: she was in Dr Tanaka's house, at the Senmonka School of Ikebana! She jumped out of bed, slid open the window. Some distance away the bell in the school grounds was ringing; a flight of pigeons rose up over a cluster of dark pine trees; the scent of blossoms came on the spring breeze.

As soon as she began to move about in her room, one of the little maidservants came hurrying to show her to the Western-style bathroom. Since the morning was fresh Valerie later chose a tweed skirt with a Shetland sweater, both in a deep hyacinth blue that echoed her eyes and made her fair hair seem fairer still. This was not done with any conscious desire to play up her blonde good looks in a country of dark-haired people, but when she saw the astonishment in the eyes of the other students at the school, she realized she had created quite a sensation.

The day at the Senmonka School began with ten minutes of silent thought: it was to this that the bell had summoned her, but Valerie had slept too late. Dr Tanaka was coming out of the hall with his students, who covered a wide age-group.

' Ah, Valerie, did you sleep well?'

' Yes, thank you, Dr Tanaka. I'm sorry I overslept.'

' Nonsense, I told my wife to leave you. Breakfast now—it is waiting. This way.' He led her through a courtyard to the side of the house, where a partition had been opened to make a patio breakfastroom looking on to a paved garden with a porch and a group of carefully-trained dwarf maples.

' By the way, a Mr Cummings rang before you were awake, to ask if you had arrived safely.'

' Oh, yes—'

' I assured him you were well. What a good friend, to be so anxious. He is known to your family?'

' Well, actually, no. I only met him two days ago.' Then hastily, seeing disapproval in Dr Tanaka's face, ' He is very kind, very respectable— I'm sure my parents would not object.'

It was only afterwards she realized that she had been near to apologizing to Dr Tanaka for making friends with a man her parents didn't know. If she could be so quickly influenced, how difficult it must be for a Japanese girl to assert her independence.

The day's classes began immediately after breakfast, which Valerie shared with the Tanaka family; the other resident students ate in a communal dining-hall on the far side of the courtyard. There were some non-residents, European and American, who had rooms at a small hotel. Dr Tanaka lectured in both Japanese and English, explaining the basic rules of Ikebana flower arrangements and the philosophical principles behind them. Then there was a demonstration by one of his assistants, with a commentary. Following this materials were distributed to each student, seated at a low table, and each was left to reproduce the lines just demonstrated by Miss Ayama.

This was by no means easy. Valerie had already attended lectures in England so that she understood the basic aim, but when she watched the delicate balance of proportion and line achieved by Michiko on one side and an elderly Japanese male on the other side, she began to despair. They were all using pussy-willows for the main uprights, and no matter how carefully she studied and pruned the twigs, hers still had an ungainly look.

She was still struggling with the three main stems when a tiny gong was struck, and she discovered it was lunch time.

'Did you do well today?' Mrs Tanaka inquired politely as she sat down to lunch.

'No, very badly.'

Dr Tanaka smiled at her. 'It will come,' he said. 'First it is necessary to calm the mind—flowers do not obey hands that are tense and over-anxious. Your little friend, Michiko-*san*—she is much more relaxed.'

'Maybe she just has more talent?' Valerie suggested.

'I do not think so. Eat now, and afterwards rest. This afternoon do not come to the class. Go for a walk, look at the cherry trees, let your mind drink in their beauty. Then tomorrow you can begin again.'

Valerie was tempted, but the idea of going out alone was rather alarming. She could not speak Japanese, and as for reading the street-signs—they were incomprehensible to her. Suppose she got lost—?

'Could Michiko come with me?' she asked.

'Certainly, if she wishes.'

Michiko had brought a packed lunch, which she was eating in the shelter of a grove of willows at the far end of the grounds. When Valerie sought her out to propose a sightseeing tour that afternoon, she looked a little dubious.

'Dr Tanaka will not like it if I do not attend the lecture . . .'

'He said you could come, Michiko.'

'Yes, but I have not so much time as you, Valerie, so I don't wish to miss lectures.'

Valerie was wondering whether she should try to

13

persuade her when a voice hailed them, and Kan came running across the hillside to meet them.

'Good afternoon! My father tells me he has given you a free afternoon, and I too am free—I have an essay to write, but I can do that this evening. Can I be your escort?'

'Oh, Kan, would you? I was trying to persuade Michiko, but she doesn't think she should.'

He turned to Michiko. 'Do come,' he urged. 'The blossom is coming out at Kiyomizudera—you would like it.'

'I ought not—'

'Why not? To look at cherry-blossom is part of learning about flowers!'

'I will come,' Michiko said.

And something in the way she spoke told Valerie that it was not the promise of the opening blossom but Kan's company that made Michiko agree.

The idea delighted her. They were such a beautiful couple—both slim and supple, Michiko's head almost reaching Kan's shoulder, her timid good manners toning down his boisterous *joie de vivre*. Though they were both exquisitely attentive to her, Valerie found opportunities to walk a little apart during the afternoon, and was pleased to see Kan talking gently to the girl as she stood, head bent, hands folded, the very picture of the well-brought-up maiden.

Kiyomizudera, Valerie was told, meant Temple of the Pure Springs, so called because of the waterfalls in the temple grounds. The Community (for there were several shrines and chapels, as well as restaurants and little shops) was in the hills east of Kyoto, clustered atop a ravine with steep sides. A terrace had been built out over the ravine for *hanami*—flower-viewing. Down below was a sea of brown branches tinged with the blush of the budding cherry: breathtakingly beautiful, dizzying in its sweep of distance that reached on and on until the eye lost the power of focus. On the other side there was a pagoda, triple-storeyed, gleaming scarlet in the cool sunlight of late March.

' We must come back in a week's time,' Kan said. ' The blossom will be open then.'

' Yes,' Valerie agreed, unwilling to talk after so much beauty.

They had tea at one of the stalls. Kan, irrepressible as ever, talked on about next week's *hanami* picnic; Michiko made gentle little sounds of agreement. Valerie was not expected to take part and was glad of that. Dr Tanaka had been right; she had needed something to check the continued excitement and activity of her journey here. Now, she felt, she had at last come close to the heart of Japan. She had had her first glimpse of cherry-blossom.

Kan drove them back, stopping to drop Michiko at her uncle's. And this time it was impossible to refuse their hospitality: ' It would be impolite,' Kan whispered. So they went in, were introduced to Tori Misumi and his wife and two small sons, and were served glasses of orangeade. Valerie realized they were very honoured to have the son of Dr Tanaka,

15

Principal of the Flower School, call on them.

The maids were scurrying about with trays of crockery when she and Kan reached home. 'To-night we are having European dinner, in your honour,' Mrs Tanaka explained. 'You like steak?'

'Steak?' Kan echoed. 'I *love* it! What a pity we didn't bring Michiko home with us, Valerie—she told me she liked European food.'

'Michiko?' said his father, looking up over his glasses.

'We took her with us to see the cherry trees.'

Dr Tanaka said something in Japanese which sounded as if he were saying 'Indeed?'

'She is a friend of Valerie's,' Kan said defensively.

'That is true. I hope she enjoyed the outing, and our guest also.'

'Oh yes, it was glorious!' Valerie exclaimed.

So the moment of faint discord passed off, and she dismissed it from her mind.

As the week progressed it was borne in upon her that the Tanakas were really very high up the social scale—much higher in their own community than Valerie's parents were in theirs. Dr Tanaka was clearly something of a celebrity; the school was famous and brought in a great deal of money. The domestic quarters were beautifully furnished, with enough European pieces to give comfort without clutter.

There were two maids (who worried Valerie because they seemed only about thirteen years old, though she had no way of checking this because she spoke no Japanese and they no English). There was also a cook and an old man who swept the paths and picked up the litter. There was a gardener and a gardener's boy. At the school there was a cook and a cleaner. The teaching staff consisted of two chief assistants and two junior assistants.

Added to this there were the students at the school, who treated Dr Tanaka with a respect bordering on awe. It was no wonder, then, that here in his own domain he was not quite the same diffident figure he had seemed when she met him in Manchester; he had about him now an aura of prestige and esteem which even Kan paid some homage to.

For instance, Kan took time off from lectures, but did not let his father know. Kan went out sightseeing or to the cinema with Valerie and Michiko, but did not give his father the fullest account of these expeditions. Kan would 'happen to meet them' when they were out buying flowers for a special assignment, but he omitted to say so to his father.

It was none of Valerie's business. What Kan told or did not tell Dr Tanaka was no concern of hers.

That much was true. But soon she found herself actively playing a part in this little comedy, because it appealed to her romantic heart. For it was quite plain to her that Kan and Michiko were attracted to each other—and nothing, in her opinion, could have been nicer. 'Very *modan*,' she told herself with a smile, as she watched Michiko glow in the pleasure of being admired by a young man whom her mother had scarcely met. *Modan* was the Japanese version of ' modern ', and it meant free, emancipated.

It was all suitable: a pretty, intelligent girl and a handsome, clever young man. No Japanese matchmaker, of the kind traditionally employed, could have done better, she felt sure.

The days had gone with such dream-like speed that a week had passed before she knew it. And still she hadn't phoned Clark Cummings! It was really too bad of her. On Saturday morning she asked Mrs Tanaka to get the number for her, and when the connection was made asked for ' Cummings-*san*.'

Almost at once his voice said, ' *Tadaima!* Anybody home?'

It seemed an odd thing to say on the telephone. But Mrs Tanaka was pulling at her elbow and pointing, and there was the explanation—Clark and Toby were crossing the courtyard towards the porch of the Tanaka's house.

' Clark!' she exclaimed. She hung up, to turn in explanation to Mrs Tanaka. ' This is the friend I was trying to phone!'

' *Mosimosi!*' cried Mrs Tanaka, hurrying out to greet them. ' Valerie was telephoning you! How pleased we are to see you. Come in, come in!'

Clark returned her bow, smiling past her at Valerie. Toby neatly sidestepped her to take Valerie's hand in his.

' Told you we'd come!' he said. ' We've got business at Toba Bay.'

One of the maids had gone to inform Dr Tanaka, who was in his study. After the formal introductions, a holiday note began to prevail; Kan was already getting the car out for an excursion to see the blossom, while the cook was bringing baskets of food to load on board.

'You must come too,' Kan insisted. 'You don't have business today?'

'No fear,' Toby said. 'Saturday and Sunday are days of rest—aren't they, slave-driver?'

'If we can manage it,' Clark said. 'I enjoy a day off as much as you do, Toby, but it's not always possible if people want to have a meeting.'

Valerie thought he looked tired. 'It would do you good to come on the picnic,' she coaxed. 'We'd love to have you both—wouldn't we, Doctor?'

'Honoured,' Dr Tanaka said, bowing.

So it was settled that Clark and Toby should follow in Clark's car. 'Where are we going?' Clark inquired as an afterthought.

'To Arashiyama.' Kan went to lean against Clark's door, to give him directions, or so it seemed. But a few minutes later, when Clark drew up at the Misumis' house, Valerie realized he'd been arranging to call for Michiko. If Clark hadn't turned up, it would have been impossible to include her, for the Tanaka family car would only carry four. But Clark's Honda had two spare seats, so Michiko was added to the party together with the elder of her two little cousins, a solemn little boy of ten in dark blue jeans, windcheater, and a baseball cap.

The weather today had turned much warmer, bringing out scores of *hanami* parties. Valerie had had no idea that cherry-blossom could call forth almost as big a crowd as a football match, but so it proved. If she had gone to a beauty spot in England and found it so crowded, she would have been vexed; here it all seemed to add to the fun.

Dr Tanaka explained that they must make their way down to the river, the River Oi, and then they would be able to see the cherry trees planted by the Emperor Kameyama in the thirteenth century. ' Notice how the maple makes a contrast to the pale pink of the blossom. Let your eye become accustomed to the subtle shades of green—there are pines and spruce there, and willow by that bank.'

' Did we come for a picnic or a lecture?' whispered Toby in her ear.

' S-sh!' she scolded.

Dr Tanaka, well launched now, analysed the various factors that made such a pleasing picture: the wide expanse of water reflecting the varied greens, the contrast of pink and bronze from the cherry and the maple, the shadows, the grey of the rocks, and so on, and so on. The grown-ups owed him the politeness of appearing to listen; the little boy, unaware that this was one of the most respected men in his town, wandered off to find amusement.

All at once Michiko sprang up with a cry. ' *Itoko!* Little cousin!' She was already running to stop him, but it was too late. Young Noburu had clambered aboard one of the boats drawn up by the jetty, and was pushing it off with the long pole used for propulsion. No one else was on board; the boatman was at a stall some yards away, buying tobacco.

Clark raced along the jetty, took a flying leap across the six feet of water between boat and quay, and landed in a sprawl in the narrow stern. Noburu, backing away, fell over the plank seat and let go the pole; it went floating off on the stream.

Kan gave a shout of laughter and went sprinting off to fetch the boatman who was already on his way at sight of his precious craft being mishandled. Together they jumped into the next boat, poled out, retrieved the other pole, and came alongside the drifting sampan. In a moment both boats were back at the shore.

Michiko took Noburu by the hand to bring him ashore. She was scolding him, but very gently. Mrs Tanaka leant down to wag a finger at him, but no one seemed inclined to be cross; Valerie had noticed that no one ever seemed to be angry with a child.

Grinning, Clark was dusting himself off. ' That was a great rescue scene,' he observed. ' He and I nearly got marooned together. Hey, listen—that wasn't a bad idea of the kid's—why don't we hire a boat?' He stooped to speak to the little boy in Japanese; for answer he received a beaming smile and a vehement nod. ' Right, that's the plan, then —who wants to go for a look at the cherry-blossom from the water?'

It seemed everyone wanted to go, and two boats

were needed. Somehow, when they were all settled, it had happened that Valerie and Michiko were together with Toby and Kan in one sampan while Dr and Mrs Tanaka were with Clark and little Noburu.

' Hard *luck*, old man!' crowed Toby as their boat sped past Clark. ' You don't seem at your best on a boat!'

Although Valerie enjoyed the outing, she couldn't help having twinges of uneasiness. Would it be considered impolite to have gone off leaving the Tanakas like that? Michiko too seemed a little uneasy; her little cousin was her responsibility, so she should have kept him with her. The boat glided close against the rocks where the pines overhung to make a dense, sweet-smelling canopy; the boatman sang to himself as he poled them gently along; the sun shone, the birds sang . . . And yet Valerie was glad when they were back at the riverbank again.

It was some fifteen minutes before the other boat came back. They needn't have worried. Noburu was hanging over the side gleefully ' catching fish' with a net fashioned for him by Dr Tanaka out of grass-stems; Clark was hanging on to the back of his trousers to keep him from falling in while Mrs Tanaka looked on, smiling indulgently.

The rest of the day was spent idly sauntering about Arashiyama in the sunshine. Noburu had adopted Clark as an honorary uncle, and because he stayed near him Michiko did too; her conscience was troubling her. Kan stayed with Michiko . . . so in effect the party lost its tendency to split into little groups.

As they made their way back to the car park Kan inquired where the wto men were staying in Kyoto.

'We're at the Sakaki Hotel,' Clark said. 'Our firm has a permanent booking there, because overseas members are often in Kyoto. We go across to Toba Bay from here to look at the pearls.'

'The Sakaki?' Michiko said, overawed. She paused to explain to Valerie. 'That is the big new building at the top of the street where we bought flowers yesterday. It's very smart—very *modan.*'

'Ever been inside? No? Come and have dinner with us tonight. You too, Val,' said Toby.

Clark laid a restraining hand on her arm and spoke so as to override the last remark. He addressed Dr Tanaka. 'Doctor, would you do us the honour of dining with us tonight with Mr Tanaka?'

Dr Tanaka smiled in approval btu shook his head. 'Thank you, but I shall be tired after today's outing, and my wife also. We would rather stay at home. But if your invitation is still open to Valerie, I should be happy to think she will have such an enjoyable evening.'

And having firmly established himself as head of the family, the Doctor now proceeded to organize the car journey home. Michiko and her cousin were firmly settled in beside Clark and Valerie. Kan chauffeured his parents and Toby Bates. Toby was not pleased at being boxed up with the Tanakas.

Valerie glanced at Clark as he took to the road, and discovered he was grinning. 'You can't buck the system,' he said in answer to her look of inquiry. 'Toby will have to learn that, if he wants to be any use here.'

'How exactly do you mean?'

'Look at the way everything has turned out now,' he said, chuckling. 'Toby tried to get things his own way of being too clever. Now me, I buttered up the old folks, and I end up with all the pretty girls.'

'You mean you were only polite to the Tanakas because it paid you to be?'

She was amused, yet there was a hint of real reproach in her voice. He gave her a brief regard. 'Depends how you look at it. Back home in Sydney I wouldn't have to pussyfoot around, practically asking permission to take a grown girl out to dinner. But when in Japan, do as the Japanese do. It makes things much more pleasant, both in business and social contacts.'

'Yet you tend to despise the old traditions.'

'When did I say that?'

She couldn't quite remember. 'It's implied in what you just said.'

'Have it your own way.' He drove for a while in silence, then said, in a quite serious tone, 'Would you like to live in a society where a girl has to ask permission to go out with a man?'

'No, but all that is changing. That's what strikes me as so odd about you. You pay lip service to the things that are all being done away with, yet you disregard the important things, the cultural things.'

He gave a little grin. 'I'm a right roughneck, that's for sure! Sorry I've made such a bad impression.'

When they reached the Tanakas' house, Kan made an attempt to get himself invited to the dinner party at the hotel, but was at once checked by his father. 'You already have an appointment,' he was told.

'No, I have not—'

'With your English textbooks, my son.'

Downcast, Kan murmured his goodbyes and went indoors.

'What was that about " the things that are being done away with "?' Clark whispered. 'Parental discipline will be one of the last things to go, Valerie.'

She couldn't help wondering for a moment if he was right.

The two men had business at Toba Bay which would allow them to be intermittently in Kyoto for the next couple of weeks. One or other of them was always turning up to take Valerie out, and she usually managed to include Kan and Michiko in the outing.

One evening Clark arrived to ask if she would like to go to Maruyama Park to view the cherry-blossom by moonlight. The Tanakas had already spoken of this as a 'must', so she eagerly agreed. Without wondering if Clark would mind, she turned to Kan. 'You'll come too, won't you?' she asked.

Kan was only too happy. He understood, without having it put into words, that they would stop to collect Michiko en route.

Clark said nothing. But Valerie was struck with a sudden conviction that he was displeased. His usual easygoing attitude seemed to have disappeared; he replied to her conversation politely but briefly. She found herself thinking: ' He's probably quite formidable as a businessman . . .' And then, ' I wish Toby had come. Toby is always good fun.'

Maruyama Park was entered through a great red gateway, beyond which the path sloped upward to show pavilions set among the trees, lit by the stone lanterns which were so much a feature of the Japanese landscape—hollow stone columns, sometimes beautifully carved but sometimes rough and moss-clad, in which candles or tapers could be burned.

The walks of the park were crowded with sightseers, so that the girls were in danger of being jostled. Kan automatically took charge of Michiko; they walked along together hand in hand, laughing and talking, stopping to buy sweets or to have their fortunes told by the wandering soothsayers who could look into the future by means of patterns made by magic sticks.

Clark steered Valerie through the crowd with one hand on her elbow, pointing out the famous views down the wide avenues of blossom, not full out and turned by the moonlight from rosy pink to a silvery mauve. She felt that he was trying to keep Kan in sight, but in the throng it was almost impossible—and anyway, why should he? He wasn't here in the role of chaperon, for goodness' sake!

After an hour of strolling, they at last happened upon each other. Clark suggested they should walk down through Gion, the *geisha* quarter, to Shijo Dori Avenue to find a coffee bar. Kan was in complete agreement. ' I know a place,' he said, ' where they have a jukebox with all the latest discs! '

As they passed the big department store just beyond the bridge, Michiko paused to study the spring suits in one of the windows. The others paused with her, and when they walked on it was Clark who was walking alongside Michiko, dwarfing her with his height and regulating his rangy stride to her little trotting steps.

They all went into the coffee bar, which was on the corner of a main road and one of the engaging little lanes that ran at right angles to it. The place was busy so that they could not all sit together at the tables, so Clark ushered Michiko further into the café while Kan and Valerie sat near the entrance.

Kan was in high good humour, ordering coffee with whipped cream and American cookies, putting money in the jukebox, tapping out the rhythm of the music with his spoon on the side of his cup, laughing with a bright gleam in his sparkling black eyes.

' Don't you think cherry-viewing time is wonderful?' he said. ' Everybody is so cheerful then. We Japanese, you know, we like sad things—our films and plays and novels are full of sad things. But at cherry-blossom time, we are optimistic. We are all friends together, none of that stuffy old-fashioned behaviour, no social barriers. Do you have holidays like that in England?'

Valerie laughed, ' Well, we certainly don't go on cherry-viewing expeditions—at least not to the same extent. And I suppose you could say our Bank Holidays were times when we are all friends together. But really, Kan, we're a fairly easygoing crowd in England these days. Anybody can speak to anybody, without embarrassment.'

' And marry anybody?'

' Yes, and marry anybody—so long as they're both free, that is.'

' Ah. Free of parents? Of family?'

' No, no. I meant, unmarried. Free of any legal tie to another person.'

' That's the way it should be,' Kan declared, his mobile mouth curving in pleasure.

Valerie knew very well that this was to bolster his morale over his feelings about Michiko. He had only known her two weeks and it would probably surprise his parents when he told them—as Valerie thought he soon would—that he was in love with this comparative stranger.

What would Michiko say? Valerie had no doubt that she was as much in love as Kan—perhaps even more, because her feelings ran deeper than his. She turned her head now to see what Michiko was doing at the moment, and discovered to her surprise that Clark was leaning towards her, talking very seriously. Michiko's face was hidden from view because of the way they were sitting, at a slight angle to

Valerie. But something about the droop of her shoulders told Valerie she was very distressed.

At last Kan ran out of money for the jukebox, and was ready to go. He went to collect the others; they walked back to collect Clark's car and set off for home. Although Kan was still as talkative as ever, it seemed to Valerie that Michiko was very quiet.

The school was out towards Kita Oji, but on the way they would stop to drop Michiko at her uncle's house in one of the lanes north of the university. As always, they were entreated to step inside for tea and cakes, and young Noburu—who should have been in bed—began a mock wrestling match with Clark. While the menfolk were scrambling around laughing at this game, Valerie looked round for Michiko.

She had retreated to the kitchen, where she was helping her aunt to prepare the tea. Valerie, of course, was not allowed to help; as an honoured guest she must go and sit down and be waited on. When Mrs Misumi saw that she wanted to talk to Michiko, she waved both girls into a room beyond the kitchen which seemed to be a handicraft corner, for a sewing machine held pride of place.

Michiko knelt on the floor beside it and began to turn the handle this way and that aimlessly.

'Are you all right, Michiko?'

'Yes, thank you. Quite all right.'

'Have you a headache or something?'

'No, I am all right.'

' But you're so quiet.'

' I feel quiet.'

' Kan says cherry-blossom time is a time for cheerfulness.' She knelt on the matting beside her friend. ' What's the matter, Michiko?'

' Nothing, nothing,' Michiko said, turning her head away.

' Was it something Clark said?'

The other girl put up one hand to shield her face— but not before Valerie had caught the glint of tears.

' What did he say, Michiko?'

' He said . . . he said . . . that I was wicked and bad!'

And poor Michiko put her face in her hands and began to sob.

CHAPTER II

Valerie couldn't believe her ears. ' He said *what*?'

' That I was a bad girl—and oh, Valerie, he was right! My mother would be so angry with me if she knew . . .' Michiko wiped tears away with her finger-tips.

Valerie did not pretend to misunderstand. ' You mean because we've been going out with Kan? Oh, nonsense, Michiko! It's all been perfectly respectable. There's always been someone else with you.'

' That is not what I mean, or what Clark-*san* meant. It is the feeling *here*.' She laid her hand on her vivid green wool dress over her heart. ' It is wrong to have this feeling.'

' But why? Kan is a nice boy—no one could be nicer. Your mother couldn't possibly disapprove of Kan.'

' But if she knew *his* parents would disapprove?'

' What a silly idea! Why on earth should they? Is that what Clark said?'

' No, he did not say that. He did not need to. He told me to remember that I was here to stay with my uncle for only a few weeks, that soon I must go back to my mother's house in Tokyo and I must not do anything that would cause her distress.'

' I never heard anything so Victorian!' Valerie cried. ' You haven't done anything except go out sightseeing and twice to the cinema. Your mother let you come out with Toby and Clark and me in Tokyo.'

'That is true.'

'She would have let you come out with Kan, too.'

'I don't think so, Valerie.' Michiko shook her head, and added with painful honesty, 'I don't think she would let me *now*.'

'Now that you're in love with Kan, you mean?'

Michiko coloured. 'I am very wicked,' she said. 'Clark-*san* was right. Japanese girl does not fall in love.'

'But Japanese girl *has* fallen in love,' Valerie rebuked her gently. 'And why not, with Japanese boy who loves her in return?'

'You think so? Oh, Valerie, you think so?' Michiko blushed and smiled through her tears.

'I know it. Goodness, anyone only has to see you together to know it. I can't understand why Clark had to interfere,' she added in anger. 'Upsetting you like this over nothing! Who does he think he is?'

Michiko got to her feet. 'He is a good man,' she said. 'He was right to speak. Truly, my mother would not approve of my behaviour—it has been too *modan*. One daughter already made *modan* marriage and gone a long way away. My mother would not like younger daughter to be close friend with a man unless she chose him.'

'But she wouldn't object. Why should she object

to Kan?' Valerie insisted.

Michiko sighed. 'You don't understand. Maybe all right, my mother would say, "Kan is a fine young man." But if Kan's parents don't like him to be friends with me, then that is a disgrace to my mother. She loses respect of herself.'

'But it doesn't matter what your parents or his parents say,' said Valerie. 'If you love Kan and Kan loves you, what can they do about it?'

Michiko began to say something, then sighed and shook her head. 'I must help my aunt. She will wonder why I am so lazy. And you must come and drink *o-cha* or she will be offended.'

Not for the first time, Valerie wished that the Japanese laws of hospitality were a little less stringent, but she obediently followed Michiko back to the main room, where the tea party was in full swing. Clark was deep in a Japanese conversation with Michiko's uncle, for which Valerie was grateful because she didn't really know if she could have been civil to him.

At the end of half an hour polite convention had been satisfied and it was time to go. It had been understood that Clark would drive Kan and Valerie back to the school, but she felt she couldn't bear to be in his debt even to that extent.

'I think I'd like to walk back,' she said.

'Walk?' Kan said, astounded. 'It's nearly two kilometres!'

'I'd like the exercise.'

'But we've been walking all evening!'

'You don't have to walk if you don't want to, Kan.'

But of course he did. 'I should enjoy it, if *you* would,' he said.

Clark, puzzled, waved goodbye and drove off back to the centre of town where his hotel was situated. Kan and Valerie walked down the lane to the main road.

'Now,' Valerie said, 'we can take a streetcar if you don't want to walk.'

Kan stared at her. 'But then why did we not take the lift in Clark's car?'

'I can't stand that man!' she said.

So they took the streetcar to Kita Oji Bridge and walked the few yards to the Senmonka School from there. Kan had plenty to talk about; he was planning an outing for all of them to Nara next Sunday.

'You do know,' Valerie said suddenly, 'that Michiko only has one more week? She goes back to Tokyo a week on Saturday.'

They were crossing the bridge over the stream that formed part of the school's boundary. Kan paused to look down at the sparkling water. His earlier mood of elation had gone. He suddenly looked very young.

'I know,' he said, his face sombre.

Valerie turned over some phrases in her mind. 'What are you going to do? You are going to speak to her, aren't you?' But none of them seemed things she could say to a young man she scarcely knew. So at last she murmured, 'We have a saying

34

in English, Kan: "Faint heart never won fair lady." '

He nodded without looking up. She wondered if his English, excellent though it was, would be equal to the cryptic message in the proverb. After a moment's hesitation she laid her hand on his arm, and he covered it with his own.

A sharp voice spoke in Japanese. Guiltily they sprang apart, as if they had been doing something wrong. It was Dr Tanaka.

'So you are here,' he said. 'It is very late. We were wondering what had happened to you.'

Sighing, Valerie glanced at her watch. It was twenty minutes to ten. Obviously it was expected that young lady guests would be safely indoors by now. While Kan murmured apologies, they followed his father up to the house.

Next day was Saturday, and the next Sunday. Sunday was the day of the great expedition to Nara, which Kan had been planning for days. It was to be an all-day affair, for there was an enormous amount to see, the two main attractions being the giant statue of the Buddha known as the Daibutsu, and—the event that interested Valerie most—the Flower-Offering Ceremony at Yakushiji Temple.

Kan said seriously to Valerie on Saturday afternoon, 'I hope you have recovered your temper with Clark-*san*.'

'Recovered my temper?'

'You were quite mad at him last night. But I hope it was only temporary? Because I had already

35

arranged with him that we should use his car tomorrow, and if you are not going to talk to him, this will make things very difficult.'

It was all said so earnestly that Valerie burst out laughing. ' I may bring myself to exchange a few polite phrases with him,' she said.

He looked relieved. ' That's great. To tell the truth, my father would not be pleased if we broke off our good relations with Clark. He has high respect for him.'

' No accounting for tastes,' Valerie muttered to herself.

' What did you say?'

' Nothing, nothing. So we're using Clark's car for tomorrow?'

' Yes, and my father's car, which gives us eight places. Clark and I will drive, and there'll be my mother and father, you and Michiko, so that leaves two seats. I wonder if we should invite Michiko's aunt and uncle?'

' We couldn't very well do that without taking their two little boys, too, and we haven't got room.'

' Oh, they could always get someone to take the children for the day. It would be a polite thing to do, to invite them—don't you think so?'

Valerie didn't know whether Japanese parents were likely to accept invitations that would take them away from their children all day; on the whole she thought not, for few English families would do it, she felt, and Japan was a country where children were adored.

'Whose car will they go in?' she speculated.

'Oh, it had better be in Clark's car,' Kan said at once. 'He won't mind.'

This seemed to imply that the Tanakas *would* mind, but Valerie didn't think it mattered much; she was fairly certain the Misumis would refuse the invitation.

She was considerably startled, though, when Michiko herself declined to go.

'But, Michiko, I thought it was all settled!' she cried. 'Last night we were all discussing it—!'

'I did not know then that my aunt and uncle were taking me to see relatives in Otsu. I am sorry, Valerie,' Michiko said, looking away, 'but it would not be proper to refuse to go with my uncle.'

Valerie wasn't satisfied with this excuse. 'You're doing this because of what Clark said,' she accused. 'You think you ought not to go with Kan.'

This was all much too blunt and direct for Michiko, who coloured deeply and let her hand flutter to her face in that well-known gesture of embarrassment. She made no reply.

'Oh, Michiko! For goodness' sake! Don't let a few disapproving remarks from a comparative stranger spoil your fun. Of *course* you're coming to Nara!'

But she was not. Pliant and submissive she might appear, but when she felt bound by a duty nothing could shake her; she had promised her aunt and uncle to go to Otsu, and that was the end of it. When Valerie told Kan the news, he didn't even try to argue about it. ' If they have arranged the visit, she must go,' he said. A little later he had an alarming thought. ' If Michiko does not come, then we shall have no need of Clark and his car. My father will wonder why I asked him to come at all . . . I think I will phone Clark at his hotel and ask him to bring Toby.'

' Yes, do,' Valerie said with some relief. ' Toby would be a decided asset.'

When Clark arrived on Sunday morning he had brought not only Toby but Mr and Mrs Ruko, Japanese members of the firm of Lustre Jewels. They were designers of jewellery, a middle-aged couple who at once got on good terms with Dr and Mrs Tanaka, thus apparently putting Clark even higher in their estimation. The older people and Clark seemed to drift off into deep conversations in Japanese, leaving Toby, Valerie and Kan to form a separate group speaking English. Valerie didn't regret it; she felt she had little to say to Clark—she still hadn't forgiven him for upsetting Michiko, though Clark in his usual easy-going way seemed quite unaware of her disapproval.

Kan wasn't his usual talkative self, although he was always ready with information when applied to by Valerie and Toby. Their first visit at Nara was to be the Daibutsu, the ' Great Buddha '. ' He is fifty-three feet in height,' Kan told them, ' and the statue was covered with gold which was found in Japan in a northern region just at that time—this was taken to mean that it was a great blessing for us to have this statue. It was completed in 749.' He sighed. 'But of course nothing is ever completely wonderful. An earthquake damaged the statue in 855, and during a war about three hundred years later, parts of it were melted when the monastery burned down. Life is like that, isn't it? Just when everything looks right, it starts to go wrong.'

'What's the matter with *him*?' Toby whispered. 'He sounds as if he's got the blues.' Toby was very quick to sense an atmosphere.

'Well, Michiko isn't here,' Valerie pointed out.

'Oh? Like that, is it?' Toby smiled a little, his light brown eyes sympathetic but amused. 'From the way he's talking, you'd think they were parted for ever!'

'Maybe that's how it feels to him.'

They dutifully admired all the wonders of the monastery where the great statue was housed, the Great Gate guarded by two giants armed with thunderbolts, the statue of the Goddess of Mercy in another hall, her head adorned with a diadem of jewels. It was Clark who came forward with information about this. 'The headdress is of silver,' he said, 'by an artist who has never been equalled—don't you agree, Mr Ruko?'

Mr Ruko bowed assent, but spoke little English so said nothing.

'There are said to be twenty thousand pearls in the headdress,' Clark added. 'This little hall, called the Sangatsudo, must hold more than a million pounds' worth of jewellery, I should think.'

'There's no need to be so commercial about it,' Valerie said rather tartly, and felt rather than saw the look of surprise he gave her.

The Flower-Offering Ceremony, which Valerie was particularly interested to see, was in a temple in quite a different part of Nara, so after a picnic lunch in the Isui-In Garden they all climbed into the cars once more and set off to the south-west of the town.

Rather to her disappointment, Valerie discovered that the flowers in the Flower-Offering Ceremony were paper flowers; the hall, though beautiful to look at in its ceremonial decorations, did not have that cool fresh smell that she had been expecting. She preferred the view outside, the pagoda soaring up from a sea of pink and orange azaleas in bloom under a warm April sun.

There was a lake not far from the temple. While the others lingered to admire a trio of bronze statues ' completed in 696 ', as Kan explained, Valerie wandered off alone to watch the bright-feathered ducks darting in and out among the reeds. She had been sitting there some minutes, lost in thought, when she became aware that someone had come up behind her.

She turned. It was Clark. Perhaps some glint of annoyance showed momentarily, for he said: ' Am I disturbing you? I'll go away again if you like.'

She shrugged, ' Stay if you want to.'

Perhaps he thought it a grudging reply, for after a moment she heard his footsteps receding. She looked round in time to see his tall, rangy figure about halfway up the slope towards the pagoda. Then as she watched he turned, looked at her, and strode back, his face grim, his green-flecked eyes dark with anger.

'Would you mind telling me why you're so vexed with me?' he demanded. 'You've hardly said a civil word to me all day.'

She raised her brows. 'You can hardly expect me to feel very kindly disposed towards you, after what you said to Michiko.'

After a moment's surprised hesitation, he sat down on the stone bench beside her. 'What did I say to Michiko?'

'You told her she was a wicked girl. And if there ever was a grotesque misjudgement,' Valerie said hotly, 'it was that!'

'Is that what she told you? That I said she was wicked?'

'Well, didn't you?'

'Hardly,' he said.

'Are you saying she lied to me?'

'Not at all. By the time she spoke to you about it, her own guilt feelings had heightened the criticism she sensed in my words. All I said to her was that I doubted if her mother would approve of her behaviour since she left home.'

'Why shouldn't her mother approve of Michiko's behaviour? She's been doing nothing wrong!'

'It depends whose standards you're judging by. Mrs Misumi would be very unhappy indeed if she knew that her daughter was becoming more and more involved every day with a young man Mrs Misumi scarcely knows and who is, anyhow, quite outside their social range.'

'Their social range?' Valerie repeated, her tone heavily ironic. 'That's a very contemporary, twentieth-century attitude, I must say! Kan and Michiko are not tied down by any old-fashioned conventions like that. If you want my opinion, they're ideally suited.'

'It's not your opinion that counts,' he replied. 'It's the opinion of the two families. And they're aware, even if you are not, that Kan and Michiko are *not* ideally suited.'

'How can you talk such nonsense? Kan is a very handsome, clever young man. Michiko is a very beautiful, intelligent girl. He's studying English and will probably get a good job afterwards. She speaks good English and works for a fashionable boutique on the Ginza. They both have a Western outlook on life. What two people could be better matched?'

He shook his head and turned away from her for a moment. Then he swung back to say forcefully, 'I'll try to explain it to you, but you're so carried away with your own romantic notions you probably won't take it in. Valerie, by encouraging those two kids to fall in love you're doing them a great wrong. Nothing but unhappiness can come of it. Mrs Misumi would never allow it if she were here because she knows, even better than I do, that the Tanakas don't think Michiko is suitable.'

'Not suitable? Why ever not?'

'She's not good enough. Kan is the son of a very well-known man. His family are the equivalent of your old " landed gentry ". He is being educated at considerable expense, and he'll take a place in society where Michiko would not fit in. The Tanakas would be horrified if they knew Kan was seriously attracted to such an unsuitable girl.'

'But . . . but . . . I never heard anything so silly! The Tanakas *like* Michiko! They invite her to their house—they're always pleased to see her.'

'They invite her because she's your friend and *you* are their guest. The laws of hospitality require them to welcome her. But they don't treat her as an equal.'

'They do. They certainly do. They're always extremely polite to her.'

Clark wrinkled his brow in exasperation. 'Of course they're polite to her! They'd lose face if they were vulgarly rude to her.' He paused. 'It isn't fair to lord it over you because I speak the language and you don't—no one could expect you to pick up more than a word or two in this short time. But if you knew a little Japanese you'd realize that they have a system of " respect " phrases. It all graduates down depending on how much respect you feel towards the person you're speaking to or about. You've heard of this?'

'Ye . . . es,' Valerie said unwillingly. 'It all sounds terribly complicated to me.'

'Take my word for it, it's a nightmare for foreigners. But if you understand a little about it, it can give you a lot of clues to what people are really thinking. And this I can assure you, Valerie—when Kan's father and mother speak about Michiko in Japanese, they speak about her as an inferior. And when they speak *to* her, they address her as an inferior. And, Valerie—' he laid an admonitory finger on her arm—'Michiko accepts it as being right and proper. She doesn't think of herself as being equal to the Tanakas.'

'That's all totally beside the point,' she replied in valiant retaliation. 'It's not what Dr and Mrs Tanaka think that matters. It's what Kan and Michiko think.'

She saw his angular face take on a tinge of anger. 'I've just told you what Michiko thinks. She knows she's not a suitable match for Kan Tanaka.'

'She knows nothing of the sort—'

'Stop kidding yourself!' he broke in, without gentleness. 'What's more important, stop trying to kid Michiko. Her conscience is hammering at her until she doesn't know what she's doing, but one thing's certain—she would never marry Kan or get engaged to him without the consent of both families.'

'I'm sure you're exaggerating! The Tanakas aren't so hidebound as that. They'd say yes, once Kan explained how he feels.'

'They would not,' Clark said. 'They would *not*. They would tell him to behave responsibly and wait until they select a suitable wife.'

44

'You're joking!' she gasped. 'Select a wife for Kan?'

'It's the way it's usually done, and—'

'But that's a thing of the past, surely! I mean, a man with Kan's intelligence and education wouldn't let someone else choose his wife!'

'It happens all the time,' he insisted. 'I hear a lot of fellows telling me how " *modan* " they are, but when it comes to the serious things in life they fall back on tradition.'

'Then you ought to be on my side in this,' Valerie flared, 'because you despise tradition.'

'On your side?' he echoed. 'You mean it's a battle? I thought we were talking about the happiness of two people you regard as friends.'

She opened her mouth to reply but, shamefaced, fell silent. Clark watched her for a moment and then said: 'Kan and Michiko have only known each other a couple of weeks. You wouldn't expect two English people to be sure of what they feel for each other in so short a time, yet you want this pair to come to a decision, overcoming all sorts of inhibitions and opposition to do it. Don't you think you're being unreasonable?'

She rallied her thoughts. She was sure that Kan and Michiko were in love and, that being so, they had the right to come together. 'I certainly think they would get engaged if they didn't have to take a lot of totally unimportant things into consideration. I think you were wrong to force Michiko to remember the taboos and embargoes of old-style thinking.

45

She *wants* to be modern. I don't think you have any right to make her unsure of herself.'

'Heaven give me patience,' he said harshly. 'Michiko is about twenty-two or three, brought up to believe that it's a woman's role to be subservient, to be meek, gentle, complaisant. When she's with you she feels strong and self-reliant, but years of training have conditioned her. Sure, she's tempted at the idea of being *"modan"*, but she couldn't go through with it.'

'She will if Kan asks her to!'

'But he won't. I'll take a bet in any currency you care to select—Kan Tanaka would never ask her to marry him unless his parents agreed.'

'You're wrong,' she said, 'you're so wrong.'

He got to his feet. 'You must be the blindest, silliest girl I ever met,' he said. 'And why I ever bothered whether you were vexed with me I'll never know!'

He stalked away. Astounded, Valerie stared after him, but this time he didn't turn and come back. And strange to say, she was hurt that he did not.

As the following week passed, Valerie became more and more concerned about Michiko. She was depressed and rather listless; her work in the Ikebana classes suffered, losing its poise and freshness. Where formerly an unerring instinct had prompted her how to place each leaf and petal in a *seika* arrangement of narcissi, now her small thin hand would hesitate and sometimes, in its hesitation,

46

knock down the flowers already settled.

Dr Tanaka was surprisingly patient with her, but she lost heart very easily, giving up her attempts and sitting back on her heels to watch Valerie work. Valerie, who was improving all the time, was often too engrossed to notice her friend's inactivity until it was too late to help her achieve anything before the lesson ended. Since there was nothing completed on Michiko's table, it was impossible for Dr Tanaka or his assistants to make any useful comment or award a commendation. When Michiko went back to the Tokyo boutique, she would not be carrying any message of approval to the manager who had so kindly financed her lessons.

Yet she hardly seemed to care. And when Valerie tried to talk to her, she was silent except for the most ordinary small-talk. Valerie took her out walking and on little shopping expeditions; she went willingly, gave opinions on dress lengths and kimonos, acted as interpreter—but the sparkle had gone.

After the day at Nara, Clark didn't show up again for a while. Valerie told herself irately that he was no loss, but she was the only one who thought so. Each day the Tanakas, husband and wife, would say in hopeful politeness: 'Shall we see Clark-*san* today?' Kan often mentioned him: 'If Clark would show up we could all drive to Kameoka . . .' or 'We'll go to see the Cherry Dances at Kaburenjo Theatre when Clark's available.'

Toby told them Clarke was very busy. 'He and

the Rukos are very tied up in selecting the pearls for some new designs—you'd be amazed how much discussion about size and colour goes on before a design goes into production.' Toby grinned and added, ' Mind you, I'm not complaining. It means I can have you more or less to myself!'

It was Toby who took her to see the famous Cherry Dances (*Miyako Odori*) at the Kaburenjo. For Valerie it was an evening of utter enchantment, portraying all the romantic beauty she had expected to find in Japan. The musicians sat in two long boxes on either side of the stage wearing kimonos embroidered in green and yellow, the colour of young spring leaves; the scenery, flimsy in construction, was beauifully painted and decorated, and the backcloths were like huge paintings lovingly accomplished. The kimonos, fans and parasols of the dancers were breathtakingly lovely—every shade and tint, every style of embroidery from flowers and leaves, birds and butterflies, to scenes of mountains and rivers.

Because the colour and style of the costumes was so important, the dances of necessity were slow, almost stately. The movements reminded Valerie of a willow tree in the wind. No one leapt or skipped or spun—the most vehement motion was the fluttering of a fan, the most dramatic the manipulation of a wide sleeve to hide the face coquettishly.

As the final chorus row of *geisha* bowed goodnight, the lights in the great red and white lanterns came on and the audience began to file out into the street, chattering softly in approval. Toby took Valerie's arm to guide her.

'Wasn't that fabulous?' Toby said. 'I've never seen anything so beautiful.' He smiled at Valerie. 'Did you enjoy it?'

'Oh yes, I can't tell you how much . . .' They walked in silence for a while, then she added, 'But you know . . . seeing those girls . . .'

'What?'

'Did you notice how modest and restrained they seemed? Every movement seemed to imply that they were shy and demure.'

'Of course. That's the whole essence of the performance, I imagine—to portray the perfect Japanese woman.'

'Well then, if that's true . . . maybe there was a lot of sense in what Clark said.'

'About the *Miyako Odori*? I never thought he'd ever go to see it!'

'I don't know that he did. He was talking about Japanese girls in general, and he said they were trained up from birth to be meek and gentle.'

'No argument about that.'

'Even the present-day ones?'

Toby shrugged. 'I imagine so. Some of them rebel these days, but it must take an awful lot of initiative to change your way of life after you've been sweet and gentle for eighteen or twenty years.'

'How about Michiko?' Valerie queried.

'How do you mean?'

'Would you say she has the willpower to rebel

49

against the general convention?'

'How on earth should I know?' Toby laughed. 'Anyhow, let's not talk about Michiko—let's talk about us.'

'What about us, Toby?'

'I'll have to be back in Tokyo the day after tomorrow. Can't get back to Kyoto for about eight days after that. Say you'll miss me?'

'You know I will.'

'Will you think of me all the time?'

'Not all the time,' she teased. 'Dr Tanaka insists that when we're working in class, we clear our minds of all disturbing thoughts.'

'So you find the thought of me disturbing? Now I find that very encouraging,' he said. He put an arm around her, drew her close, and kissed her gently two or three times on eyebrows, cheek and chin. 'How about that? Is that disturbing, too?'

'I must say I find it very pleasant,' she murmured, 'though Michiko would say it's very shocking.'

'Oh, confound Michiko!' Toby exclaimed, quite violently. 'Why the dickens do we have to keep on talking about her? I'm not really the least bit interested in her!'

The home-going crowd from the theatre separated around them as they stood, suddenly arguing, on the pavement at Donguri Bridge. The passers-by eyed them curiously.

'I'm sorry,' Valerie said, repentant. 'It's just

that I'm worried about her. I didn't mean to bore you.'

' You didn't, darling. I was in the wrong.'

' No, it was my fault.'

' All right, then,' Toby said, tapping her cheek with a finger, ' make it up to me by coming out with me tomorrow night.'

' Oh, Toby, I'd love to, but I can't. Michiko is taking the evening train home to Tokyo.'

' So what? She can get aboard a train without help, I imagine.'

Valerie drew away from him sharply. ' I have to be there to see her off. Saying goodbye to travellers is a big thing here, I gather. Michiko's aunt and uncle and cousins are all going, and they take it for granted that I'm going too.'

' But, Valerie, *I'm* going away at midday on Saturday. If I can't see you tomorrow night it means this is our last date.'

' I'm sorry, Toby . . .'

They didn't exactly quarrel about it, but it put a restraint on their conversation all the way home. He handed her out of the taxi at the gateway of the school, gave her a cool, brief kiss, and was driven away.

When Valerie walked up the lane to the house of Michiko's uncle next night, she found a surprise awaiting her. Clark's car was outside. Even in the midst of her distress at leaving, Michiko was glowing with gratitude.

' Clark-*san* has come with his car to drive me to

the station,' she said. ' How kind he is, Valerie!'

Valerie had to admit to herself that this was true, and tried to put aside any resentment she had felt over Clark's words to her at their last encounter.

' How did you know she was leaving tonight?' she asked him.

' Toby mentioned it. He seemed a bit put out.' He glanced at her shrewdly as he said this, and she found herself colouring. She could imagine that at the hotel last night Toby might have expressed himself forcibly, and the idea was not very pleasing. But there was nothing to be read in Clark's rugged, calm features.

' He's leaving tomorrow?' she said.

' Yes, back to the main office. There are contracts to draw up for the pearls we've been buying. It's time he did some real work,' Clark said with amusement. ' He gets into mischief if he isn't kept busy!'

Despite herself, Valerie smiled. ' You talk about him as if he were a little boy!'

' Not exactly. But he always strikes me as being a bit of a gay gallant. He's good at his job, but where his leisure hours are concerned his motto is " Think no more, lad; laugh, be jolly . . ." '

Valerie looked up, her eyes wide. ' That's from " A Shropshire Lad "!'

' Quite right.'

' But you—do you—?'

' Read poetry? Not often these days. But when I was going through the usual adolescent miseries

52

and delights, I used to read it up in my room at night —all terribly intense and fervent. You wouldn't think so to look at me, would you?' he said, tapping his craggy chin.

'And you like Housman?'

'I used to, a lot.'

'Which was your favourite?'

'"When I was one-and-twenty
     I heard a wise man say,
     Give crowns and pounds and guineas
     But not your heart away."'

She looked at him, smiling. 'And you say you don't read it these days? You've got an excellent memory.' She sighed. 'I adore Housman.'

'Ah,' Clark said. 'Now I know why you're so in love with Japan.

"Loveliest of trees, the cherry now
     Is hung with bloom along the bough . . ."'

'It's so beautiful. It always brings a lump in my throat.' Even at the memory of the lines, so hackneyed, so often quoted, and yet so deeply felt, Valerie's eyes filled with tears. Or perhaps it was anxiety and regret welling up for Michiko.

'Hi, now. Silly kid! Don't be upset . . .' Clark took her by an elbow and led her out to the verandah, where the setting sun was gilding the posts of the weathered little wooden house. He patted her shoulder.

Valerie swallowed hard, found a handkerchief, and blew her nose. 'I'm sorry.'

'Is it about Michiko?' he asked.

She nodded.

' I understand how you feel, Valerie. I did try to warn you.'

' She's so unhappy, Clark.'

' And Kan?'

' He says nothing. I don't know whether they've seen each other in the last few days. I don't *understand*,' she said in low fierce tones. ' He *does* care for her, I know he does.'

Michiko's aunt, bowing, invited them in for the inevitable tea and rice crackers. Michiko was finishing her packing; the rest of the family sat round the low table, all of them rather sad at the approaching departure.

' Maybe she could stay longer,' Valerie said suddenly. ' Clark, ask them if Michiko could stay another week or so.'

When Clark translated the question, Mr Misumi shook his head vehemently and said a few brief sentences. ' He says it's better if Michiko goes home,' Clark said. ' Kyoto is not a happy place for her.'

' Oh,' Valerie said. So her relatives knew or guessed how she felt? It seemed they shared Clark's view—that any romance between Michiko and Kan was out of the question. Valerie felt baffled. Why was it so impossible? Simply because Dr Tanaka wouldn't approve? And did that really matter so much to Kan that he would let Michiko go?

When it was time to leave for the Tokaido Line Station, they all squeezed into Clark's car; the three women in the back with the smaller of the little boys

54

on Mrs Misumi's knee, the elder boy on his father's knee in the front passenger seat. The children were excited, but the grown-ups were rather silent. At the station they found Michiko a seat, settled her in it and put her luggage in.

'Goodbye, Michiko. I'll see you when I get back to Tokyo in five weeks' time.'

'Goodbye, Valerie.' Her long lashes were jewelled with tears. Above her emerald green dress her face was like white porcelain. '*Sayonara!*'

Mr Misumi made a little speech in Japanese. Everybody bowed to Michiko and she bowed in reply. The guard signalled for the train to leave. Michiko sank back in her seat and raised a hand in farewell as the window slid past the group on the platform.

Behind one of the pillars supporting the station roof a tall thin figure was standing. As Michiko's carriage window went by the man moved forward for a moment to wait unmoving, for perhaps long enough to be seen by those on the train.

Valerie touched Clark's arm. 'Look, Clark!'

But by the time he had disengaged himself from a conversation with Mr Misumi, the figure was gone.

Valerie knew, unquestionably, that it had been Kan. Why had he not come with the Misumi family to see Michiko off? Had his parents forbidden him? If so, what did his momentary appearance mean? She was baffled by the whole affair; something that in England would have been happy and straight-forward was taking on here all the overtones of complex drama.

Clark offered her his arm as they were walking towards the station exit, but before she could take it a familiar figure came sprinting up.

' Oh, don't tell me I'm too late! ' Toby panted, breathless. ' Has Michiko's train gone? '

' Just,' Valerie said. ' I thought you weren't interested? '

' Oh, darling! ' he said apologetically. ' I was sitting in the bar of my hotel, wondering whether to go in for a lonely dinner, when it suddenly struck me I was being an idiot! If you wanted to see Michiko off, why couldn't I be there too? So I grabbed a taxi on Karasuma Avenue . . .' He put an arm round her shoulders. ' What a sad face! I hate to see you like this.'

She summoned a smile. ' I'll get over it.'

' That's right, there's no need to be depressed about it. You'll be seeing her again in a few weeks.'

The Japanese members of the group were standing around politely. Clark said in a determinedly gentle tone, ' Toby, how long are these people going to have to wait before you say " Good evening " to them? '

' Huh? Oh, good heavens, I keep forgetting. *Konban wa, Misumi-san.*' He bowed, but only in the most perfunctory manner. ' Now, Valerie, to cheer us both up—you for having to part with Michiko and me for having to part with you to-morrow—let me take you out to dinner.' He began to direct her towards the street.

The idea of going straight back to the sch[ool] [cer-] tainly didn't appeal to her at present. On the [other] hand, she would rather have liked to tell Clark about seeing Kan and ask his opinion. She ventured, ' Perhaps we could make a threesome of it. Would you like to come, Clark?'

' I have to ferry the Misumis back to their home.'

' Then come along afterwards?'

He hesitated. Toby said, ' Only thing is, I don't know where we'll be. I thought of exploring some of the side-streets for a new restaurant.'

Valerie was about to suggest that they could all meet at some prearranged point, for it would not take long for Clark to drive the Misumis home.

But before she could speak Clark said crisply: ' In that case it's goodnight.'

Valerie began to say, ' Meet us later.' But the words were lost in the flow of Japanese as Clark urged Michiko's relatives towards his car. She made one more attempt. ' Clark!' she called.

He half-turned. He was towering above the neat Japanese bodies like an elm tree amidst birch saplings. A look of vexation came over his face, and at that very moment she felt Toby kiss her lightly on the cheek and murmur, ' Come on, darling—half the evening's gone!'

She enjoyed her evening with Toby; he was good company. But she couldn't help wishing she'd had a chance to speak to Clark.

CHAPTER III

Kan seemed a lonely figure to Valerie when she saw him in the next few days. Formerly he had been noisy, bright, and as full of movement as quicksilver. Now he moved about much more slowly, as if carrying a burden. He was at the university during the day, but in the evenings when she hoped to see him he remained shut up in his room with his books.

Since Toby had left for Tokyo, this left Valerie without a companion. She stayed at home two evenings with Dr and Mrs Tanaka, but though they were kindness itself she felt she couldn't face a third evening, during which they would either watch cultural programmes on television (Noh plays, Japanese puppet plays, Gagaku music) or they would talk about Ikebana and allied arts such as pottery.

Perhaps Clark wouldn't mind acting as escort. She rang his office, or at least got one of Dr Tanaka's assistants to make the connection. But when she asked for Cummings-*san* the answer, in precise, gentle English was: ' So sorry. Cummings-*san* has gone to Osaka on business for a few days.'

' When will he be back?' Valerie asked, experiencing an unexpected sense of disappointment.

' That is not quite certain. Can I ask Cummings-*san* to ring you when he returns?'

' No, thank you, it wasn't important.'

So he'd gone to Osaka without ever mention
But she pulled herself up at that thought; why on
earth should he?

She knew that the Tanakas would be upset if she
proposed going out at night alone, and in any case
the idea didn't attract her; to be out in a city where
you don't speak the language and the very street-
signs look like pretty designs rather than words is no
fun.

She racked her brains for a way out and at last
remembered that Kan had mentioned a forthcoming
event in the hall of the university—a folk group
from America were to give a recital. She said at the
meal that evening, 'I wonder, Kan, if you'd mind
taking me to hear The Wanderers? I'm a great
admirer of theirs.'

She had by this time learned enough about
Japanese hospitality to know that a wish of this kind
had to be granted. Short of the concert being can-
celled or Kan falling ill, he would have to take her.

'I'll ring up for some tickets,' he replied, and
asked his parents if they too would like to come.

Dr Tanaka shook his head. 'I am not fond of
Occidental music,' he said. Poor Mrs Tanaka
wasn't asked if she would like to go; Valerie had
also learned by now that the Doctor's wife wasn't
expected to have opinions or wishes that differed
from her husband's.

The recital, held in the magnificent modern
assembly hall of the university, was delightful. The
Wanderers sang folk-songs from various countries,

59

even including one from Japan, to the enormous pleasure of the mainly Japanese audience.

Kan, though he had read a great deal of English poetry, had never heard of most of the numbers they sang. One, in particular, had caught his attention.

'What was that song that had the story about the runaway lovers?'

'That was "Lord Ullin's Daughter",' Valerie said. 'Wasn't it sad?'

Kan sighed. 'Have you noticed that most love songs are sad?' he said.

'I suppose so.' Impelled by a wish to get him to confide in her, Valerie said she would like a cup of coffee before returning home, so they turned their steps to a café near the Old Imperial Palace.

'I had a letter from Michiko,' she said after the kimono-clad waitress had brought the coffee. 'She says she had a pleasant journey and was met at Tokyo by her mother. She sends her good wishes to all her friends in Kyoto.'

Kan stirred his black coffee round and round, although he had put no sugar in. 'Does she . . . does she seem well?' he asked.

'She doesn't complain. She says that it seems dull at the boutique after her time of freedom here.' Valerie waited, hoping that Kan would say something, but he remained silent, staring down at his coffee cup. 'Do you think you will ever see Michiko again?' she prompted.

He shook his head without speaking.

'It seems a pity to let a pleasant friendship die

60

away,' she persisted.

Kan picked up his cup, drank all his coffee, replaced the cup exactly in the centre of the saucer, and then spoke. 'In that song they sang . . . " Lord Ullin's Daughter " . . . the girl ran away from her parents to go with her sweetheart.'

'Yes, that's right.'

Kan laughed. 'That would be too much to expect here in Japan,' he said, as if he were carrying on a casual conversation. 'I don't think we have any songs about that in Japan.'

And that, apparently, was that. Valerie tried to guess at the message he had been conveying: she thought it meant that Kan would have been willing to defy his parents but knew that Michiko would never agree. Whether he had ever discussed it with her there was no way of knowing.

They were now rather late in heading for home. The evening, which had been mild when they started out, was much cooler now so that Valerie, in a long-sleeved Tricel dress, felt chilly. Kan took off the sweater he was wearing over his shirt, to drape it round her shoulders, and put his arm round her European-fashion as they walked from the taxi to the house.

The sound of their footsteps must have alerted Kan's mother, for she opened the door for them. Her hands went in a fluttering movement to her face as she saw them side by side with their arms about each other. She made a startled exclamation which brought her husband.

Valerie drew away from Kan, but wondered what the two older people thought about Kan's sweater tied round her neck. Was that a breach of manners, as was kissing and physical closeness? Judging by the frown on Dr Tanaka's face, she was not entirely approved of, at the moment.

' You are very late, Kan.'

Kan looked at his wrist. ' It's only ten-fifteen.'

' The concert was over an hour ago, my son.'

' We went for a cup of coffee.'

' You could have had coffee at home, Kan,' his mother suggested.

' Valerie said she would like some as we left the concert. It would not be very polite, would it, to make a guest wait for something so simple as a cup of coffee?'

' No, of course not,' agreed Mrs Tanaka, looking anxiously at her husband for his approval.

Dr Tanaka's eyes were on the dark red sweater tied loosely round Valerie's neck by its sleeves. ' Oh, I nearly forgot,' Kan said, and casually untied it. Beyond him Valerie could see his father watching this action, his face now impassive.

' I'll have to be more careful in future,' thought Valerie. ' They really are so easily shocked!'

From that evening Kan seemed to recover some of his zest for life. He took Valerie dancing (European-style) the next evening, met her at lunch-time the following day to show her some travel photographs lent him by a friend, and that same evening produced tickets for a performance in English of ' As You Like

It ' at the university. On Saturday he had borrowed binoculars from another friend so that he could take her bird-watching on Mount Kinugasa, Valerie having said that this was something she did at home.

She made sure they came home from all outings at what his parents would consider a suitable hour, and remembered not to hug him or hang on to his arm as she would have done with an English boy. She realized that she was far too openly impulsive and affectionate to fit in with the local idea of good manners unless she kept a tight rein on herself.

One of the little maids had a message for her. Someone had rung her while she was out bird-watching. ' Toby-*san*?' she asked, but the maid spoke so fast that Valerie's painfully acquired few words were quite inadequate. Kan, asked to translate, reported that Toby had been ringing from Tokyo; but as Toby's Japanese was almost on a level with Valerie's, he had been unable to leave a message with Hana, the maid.

Valerie was sorry to have missed him. She wondered whether to ring him next day, but decided against it for two reasons: she would have to get someone else to get the number for her (which always seemed to make it a mammoth undertaking) and it seemed rather over-eager to ring him in Tokyo.

Next day there was a family outing to see the Silver Pavilion, another of the show-places of Kyoto. She was particularly anxious to visit the Silver Pavilion because the garden around it was claimed by many to be the most beautiful in the land. She was a little disappointed to discover that the pavilion was wood, not silver, but the gardens—beautifully landscaped, full of a myriad shades of green—were gentle and sedate. Yet, for the first time, Valerie found herself longing to see flowers growing in a garden—beds of tulips and daffodils as at home, rose bushes coming into bud. She said suddenly to Dr Tanaka, 'We use flowers in our arrangements, but where do they *grow*?'

He looked surprised. 'In truck farms, of course.'

'Truck farms?'

'I think the English term is "market garden",' Kan said.

'Doesn't anyone have a flower garden?'

'Oh yes, some people do. But in general our gardens are scenes of green moss and bushes and pools. It just happens to be the tradition. Flowers are usually grown either in pots on the verandah, or in the kitchen garden.'

When they reached home again the maid reported another phone call from Toby. She talked at great length to Kan, who said to Valerie, 'He seems to have been quite mad at Hana because you were out again. Maybe you'd better call him? I'll get the number for you.'

Since it seemed possible that Toby had something important to say, Valerie accepted Kan's offer. When Toby's hotel replied, she was told that he had gone out. The reception clerk promised to tell him as soon as he came in, and about an hour later she was called to the phone.

'Well, hello at last,' Toby said. 'Every time I try to get you, you're out. Where have you been? The maid seemed to be saying you were out with Kan.'

'So I was. How are you, Toby?'

'Oh, lonely and neglected,' he said. 'I wanted to get in touch to let you know I'll be back in Kyoto on Wednesday next. See you then, Valerie?'

'Oh, I'm sorry, Toby,' she said. 'I'm going out that evening, to a Lantern Festival.'

'With Kan, I presume?'

'As a matter of fact, yes.' Nettled at his tone, she spoke crisply.

'Well then, can I see you Thursday evening?'

'Yes, I'd love to.'

'It's a date, then. I'll call for you about seven.'

'How's Clark?'

'No idea. He's still in Osaka. It's part of his plan to make me learn the language—leave me on my own here in Tokyo. I'm fed up with it. I'll be glad to get to Kyoto again for a bit of relaxation. Well, see you on Thursday, Val.'

When Thursday came Valerie was looking forward to the evening. Although Kan was a good friend and a lively companion, it wasn't the same as someone from her own background, someone to whom one didn't have to explain catch-phrases like 'You should be so lucky!' or 'Anyone for tennis?' Valerie dressed for the occasion with care, putting on a new dress she had bought in Kyoto, of thin blue silk embroidered with daisies. She couldn't help being aware that with her fair hair and violet-blue eyes, it had more than minimum appeal.

Toby seemed to think so, when he arrived to collect her. ' Why, princess, how lovely you look!' he exclaimed, and advanced upon her.

But Valerie had at last realized that even between Europeans, demonstrative behaviour was frowned upon by her hosts. She fended him off therefore. He looked a bit put out, but turned to greet Dr and Mrs Tanaka as they came forward. Kan stood by, smiling politely as they took their leave.

The tourist season was getting under way now; a great many Americans were arriving in Kyoto for the *Odori* performances which went on until mid-May and would be followed by the pageant in honour of two of the famous shrines. From then on a continual succession of traditional celebrations would provide attractive events. So in this second week in April some of the restaurants had re-opened serving European food and providing something approaching European cabaret.

Toby took Valerie to a place advertising itself in roman lettering as ' The Moon-Viewing Balcony '. The reason for this, as she discovered, was that a verandah had been built out over the river so that it was possible to watch the silver reflection in the black waters. On each table stood a little stone lantern giving a faint, flickering light. The tables and chairs were Western style, as was the food, but the waitresses wore kimonos and from somewhere there floated the plaintive music of the *samisen*. According to a note on the menu, at nine o'clock a ' *grupa* ' (group) would arrive to play for dancing.

The food was American, so they ordered fried chicken southern-style followed by chocolate pecan pie. Toby had a lot to report about his stay in Tokyo; time flew by until, almost with surprise, they heard the dance music strike up.

' Shall we?' Toby asked, holding out his hand.

' Yes, let's.'

They danced for a while in silence. Then Toby said, ' You've been seeing a lot of Kan, I gather.'

Valerie agreed that she had.

' You like him, don't you?'

' Of course I do.'

' I thought he was Michiko's boy-friend?'

' Apparently not,' she said, rather sadly. ' I don't understand the ins and outs of it, but she seemed to think his parents didn't approve of her. So she went home.'

' Leaving the field clear for you, eh?'

' What?' said Valerie, leaning away to look up at him.

' Nothing.'

' What did you say, Toby?' She had lost the beat of the music now, and they stopped dancing, staring at each other.

' It wasn't important. Forget it. Let's dance.'

For answer she walked away from him, back to their table on the verandah. She sat down, and he followed suit.

' Now,' she said. ' What was that you said about

me and Kan?'

For a long moment he hesitated, then he burst out: 'Well, you must admit it looks a bit much! No sooner is Michiko off on the train to Tokyo than you and Kan start going around together like two love-birds. Every time I phone, you're out with him. When I tried to kiss you hello tonight, you wouldn't let me, because he was there . . .'

He ran out of accusations and under her steady gaze fell silent.

'Is that the end of my crime-list?' she inquired.

'There's no need to be so off-hand about it! I can tell you I felt pretty upset when I realized the way things were going.'

'And how are they going, according to you?'

Toby didn't recognize the danger signal in her voice. 'You're falling in love with him, that's how! And you ought to wake up before it's too late, because no good can come of it!'

'Toby, if I were falling in love with Kan—which I'm not—it would be no business of yours. What makes you think you've any right to take me to task like this?'

'Good lord . . . You must know how I feel about you, Val! I haven't been able to think of anything else since you came into my life.' He put out his hand to take hers, but she avoided his grasp. He went on placatingly: 'Don't be angry with me, Val. I had to say all this. It's been bubbling up inside me for two days now.'

'But I don't understand why, Toby. I've only

known you just over a month—exactly as long as I've known Kan. If any sort of relationship has grown up between us, surely you must realize the same thing applies with Kan.'

'I can't bear it if that's true. I want you to promise me you won't go out with him when I have to go to Tokyo again. Promise me, Val!'

She shook her head and made as if to get up, but he caught her by the arm.

'No, no—don't go! You've got to understand—'

'All I understand is that you're trying to run my life for me. I couldn't possibly—'

'I'm trying to prevent you from making a complete fool of yourself!' he said, his voice rising. 'Do you realize how it *looks*? I can't let you go on making an exhibition of yourself. I forbid you to go out with Kan Tanaka!'

Valerie took hold of the hand that was grasping her arm and prised it loose. Then she stood up. 'How dare you!' she said. 'Forbid me? I'm not some obedient little Japanese girl, you know— you've let your surroundings go to your head, Toby. I shall choose my friends for myself, without any censorship from you. And now, if you don't mind, I think I'll go.'

Toby had risen too. He stepped forward so as to block her path. 'You do as you please, then,' he said harshly. 'Make a fool of yourself over handsome Kan Tanaka. But I'll tell you this—his parents will never allow him to get seriously involved with you. They'd rather have Michiko and all her poor relations—at least she's Japanese. They certainly don't want a hard-up English flirt!'

Valerie didn't stop to think. She simply pushed Toby out of her way with a strength she didn't know she possessed, and ran out of the restaurant.

CHAPTER IV

She ran up the narrow side-street, hardly able to see because of the tears that were blinding her. Passers-by turned to stare at her, but she paid no heed. Only when she found herself gasping for breath did she stop.

She had no idea where she was. This was a part of Kyoto she had never visited before and when they had come to the restaurant they had been in a taxi which delivered them straight to the door. Traffic here was very thin; she could see no taxis and there were no streetcar wires overhead.

She stopped, leaning against a shop window to recover her breath. It was very dark in the street; the lamps were far apart and few of the shop windows were lit. She pulled herself together and walked on, looking for a sign in a window that said ' English Spoken ' (or more commonly, ' American Spoken '). In a little road like this, probably there were one-man businesses, with the owner living behind the shop, and she could perhaps knock someone up.

At the next street junction there were overhead lamps. There were one or two people about; one, an elderly man in a dark European suit and a homburg hat, was eyeing her with owlish solemnity through horn-rimmed glasses.

Taking her courage in both hands, she went up to him and bowed. ' Excuse me, sir. Do you speak

English?'

He stared at her. A slow, foolish smile dawned on his face.

'*Kin-iro*,' he murmured. '*Kin-iro*.' He put out a hand and stroked her hair.

She drew back sharply, alarmed. And then she realized that he was commenting on the colour of her hair and, furthermore, that he was rather the worse for liquor. One of the things she had noticed was that 'cherry-viewing' (like a Bank Holiday in England) was the excuse for merrymaking that sometimes ended, for the men, in a haze of *saké*, the national drink.

The last thing she wanted was to get involved with a drunken man. To avoid him she turned away, crossed the street walking rapidly, and turned a corner. A little further along lights beckoned; she hurried up to it—it was a railway station.

A wave of relief swept over her. There was a suburban line that served the vicinity of Kyoto, and she knew there was a station near the school. She racked her memory for the name of the station, but it wouldn't come. Still, she could tell the ticket man the name of the district and he would tell her the name of the station that served it.

The name of the neighbourhood was Kita-ku. She went to the ticket window and said, 'Kita-ku?', showing some money.

The man inside shook his head and produced a flood of Japanese she couldn't understand, pointing to the entrance where she had just come in.

72

She tried again. 'Kita-ku?' Then remembering the name of the streetcar stop nearest the school, 'Karasuma?'

Once again he shook his head and uttered a few sentences. Then, seeing she was totally at a loss, he left the ticket window to reappear at a door to the left. He bowed, walked in front of her making a 'Follow' gesture, and when she did so ushered her to the door and began pointing to the right up the street, indicating that she should take several turnings.

Helplessly she looked at him. Then, struck by a thought, she held out her palm and made writing guestures with the other hand upon it. Her helper's face lit up; he took her back to the ticket office, found a scrap of paper, and began to write directions on it.

But, of course, they were in Japanese characters.

With a feeling that was almost desperation, Valerie touched his wrist to stop him, held out her hands palms-up in the universal gesture of incomprehension, but produced a smile of thanks. He pushed back his cap and gazed at her, waiting for her next suggestion.

In a moment she had another inspiration. From out of nowhere she remembered the Japanese word for telephone. 'Denwa?' she asked, and made dialling and telephoning signs.

Once again his thin face broke into a beam of pleasure. He waved her ahead of him into his little office, where the telephone sat on his immaculately neat desk.

She picked it up, but then was faced with another crisis. What was the telephone number of the Senmonka School? She'd never had to ring the Tanakas; the only calls she had made were to Toby and Clark at the Sakaki Hotel. She closed her eyes and tried to picture the sequence; to her surprise it came, and without stopping to think about it she dialled. Someone at the hotel would be able to speak English, she felt sure.

The receptionist replied in Japanese. She said, 'Do you speak English?' and the girl at once answered, 'I sure do!'

Valerie almost laughed aloud in relief. But then she realized she had to explain her predicament and why on earth she was ringing the Sakaki Hotel.

'I'm a friend of Mr Clark Cummings,' she began. 'I—'

'Oh, you want to be put through to him?'

'Is he there?' But before she could get over her surprise and go on with her explanation, there was a click and Clark was saying: 'Cummings here.'

'Oh, Clark! Oh, *Clark*! Am I glad to hear your voice!'

'Valerie?' There was a fractional pause. 'What's the matter? How did you know I was back?'

'I didn't,' she confessed, almost in tears with relief. 'I just rang your hotel because it was the only number I could remember, and they put me through to you. Clark, I'm *lost!*'

'What do you mean, lost? Who's with you?'

'No one, except a nice little ticket man who doesn't speak any English.'

'Ticket man?' Clark's voice was growing more and more astounded with every word. 'Where on earth are you?'

'I've no idea, except that it's a little railway station.'

'Railway station? What are you doing alone in a railway station at this time of night?'

'Oh, Clark . . .'

'Let me talk to your ticket man—is he there?'

'Yes, he's standing beside me. Just a minute.' She offered the phone to the railway official, but he backed away saying something that obviously meant 'I don't speak English.' She nodded encouragingly, so he took the receiver and spoke into it. His face relaxed as Clark questioned him. Smiling and nodding, he gave information, then handed the phone back to Valerie.

'Right. Sit down and relax. I'll be there in ten minutes.'

Clark was as good as his word. She heard the car and the slam of the driving door, then a moment later he came striding in. He gave her a sharp glance, but once being assured she was all right he turned to give his thanks to the ticket man, who was smiling and bowing in a glow of delight.

Valerie, too, remembered her manners without any prompting. Facing the kind little man, she gave him a deep bow betokening extreme respect, and said one of her few words of Japanese: 'Arigato,

arigato.'

As they drove away, Clark said: ' We'll go to the Sakaki. You look as if you could do with a cup of good strong Australian tea.'

The traffic wasn't heavy at that hour. In no time at all they were turning into a thoroughfare she recognized. ' Why, this is Karasuma! This is where that nice little man was trying to direct me!' She glanced back the way they'd come. ' So why couldn't I go on a train to Kita-ku district?'

' Not from that station, you couldn't. It's one of Kyoto's little privately-owned railways, doesn't go any farther north than Keihan.'

' But there *is* a station near the school, isn't there?'

' Yes, but it belongs to a different company. You could never have got to it from that station.'

They pulled up at the hotel. Clark surrendered his car to the parking-boy, then led Valerie into the lounge. True to his word, he succeeded in obtaining a tea-tray carrying a European-style teapot, milk, and sugar. ' This is probably breaking their hearts,' he said, ' but I *like* tea with milk and sugar.'

He waited till she had drunk a cup—and to tell the truth, it was the most welcome thing she had been offered in days! Then he said, ' Now, what were you doing out on your own at a time of night when respectable Japanese girls are usually safe at home?'

' We . .ell . . .' She hesitated. She didn't want to get Toby into any trouble; after all, it wasn't his fault that she'd no sense of direction. 'I was out with someone, we had a bit of an argument, and I marched off in a huff.'

'Did you now? And who was with you? Kan?'

She shook her head. 'I'd rather not say.'

'Whoever it was,' Clark said, 'they shouldn't have let you wander off. The Japanese are a very law-abiding race, but they do have a criminal class, and a European woman tourist walking around on her own at night would seem fair game. Promise me you'll never do such a thing again?'

'I promise,' she said fervently.

He poured more tea for her, watching her closely. 'You're looking better now. You were quite white before. Sure you wouldn't like to tell me what it was Toby said to upset you?'

'Oh no, it was all so silly—' She broke off. 'I never said it was Toby!'

Clark sat back, smiling. 'Well, it was a sure bet it wasn't Kan. He would never have let you walk off by yourself—his self-respect would be so damaged by bad manners like that that he'd probably never survive. If it wasn't Kan, it was probably Toby, because he's the only other escort that I know of, and moreover, he isn't in the hotel— I asked for him when I arrived. So what did he say?'

'Honestly, Clark, it was nothing. I was silly to get indignant.'

'I'm not convinced,' he said. 'I know *I* made you angry that day at Nara, but from your point of view you had good reason. Still, if you don't want to tell me, you're entitled.' He glanced at her cup. ' Finished?'

She nodded, but her mind was already ranging forward. She glanced at her watch; the time was just on ten o'clock, yet here in Kyoto it felt like some wicked hour in the middle of the night. ' Dr Tanaka is going to be so shocked when I get home so late,' she lamented.

' Ah,' Clark said, smothering a grin, ' so you're beginning to be affected by the '' strong-father '' routine? Now maybe you understand how difficult it is for a girl born and bred here.' But seeing she still looked worried he said, ' Hold on here, then. Have another cup of tea or something. I'll ring Dr Tanaka and explain that you've been delayed.'

Off he went, threading his way among the low tables in the practically empty lounge. He walked with an easy co-ordinated gait that made her think he might have been happy in some outdoor career —rancher, perhaps, or forester. But he had the drive and initiative to get to the top in a big business set-up. A strange mixture—difficult to know, difficult to live up to, yet with a core of unexpected gentleness.

When he returned he was looking puzzled.

' It was Kan who answered the phone,' he said. ' I didn't give him all the details, just said you'd got a bit off the beaten track and got lost but I'd bring you home in about fifteen minutes. He *insisted* on coming out to collect you himself.'

'Maybe he felt it was required of him?'

'Maybe,' Clark agreed. 'I know a bit about the social conventions, but of course I don't always catch all the nuances . . . I'd have thought he'd have been satisfied if I brought you home, though. After all, if a European takes you out and behaves thoughtlessly to you, Kan's honour isn't affected . . . Oh well, it's no good kidding myself I know all the answers.'

Valerie was a little perturbed. Why should Kan turn out—at what to his parents must seem the middle of the night—to fetch her home, when she already had a willing and totally respectable escort? It didn't make sense. It would mean an awful lot of embarrassing explanations to his parents when she got back.

They were still sitting waiting for him when Toby walked into the lounge.

'My God, so there you are! I've been half out of my mind with worry!' he exclaimed, hurrying over.

'So you damn well should be,' Clark said coldly. 'I ought to knock your teeth in!'

'Please, please,' Valerie soothed, looking from one to the other. 'I'm here and I'm quite all right.'

'You mean you've been here while I've been running round Kyoto looking for you, and ringing the Tanakas to see if you'd got home?'

'You rang the Tanakas? When?'

Toby glanced at his watch. 'About twenty minutes ago.'

'Kan didn't mention that,' Clark murmured.

'Was it him you spoke to?'

'No, one of the maids, then I asked for Dr Tanaka.'

'Did you tell him what had happened?'

'Well, no . . .' Toby looked embarrassed. 'I just said Valerie and I had got separated and I wanted to know if she'd got home.'

'And then when I tell Kan I've found her, he's determined to fetch her himself. Sounded in quite a state.'

Toby scowled, and Valerie felt colour flooding up into her face. Clark studied them in a moment of dispassionate silence. 'I suppose somebody knows what's going on,' he remarked. 'I feel like an actor who's been pushed on stage without knowing what play he's in . . .'

A moment later Kan arrived, his thin face very worried. 'Valerie, are you all right? When my father gave me Toby's message—!'

'I'm perfectly all right,' she said. 'It was my own silly fault.'

'We must go now. Thank you, Clark, for taking charge of the situation.' He bowed. 'I am in your debt.'

This last phrase was one Valerie had heard more than once; it seemed to be an almost literal translation of some Japanese idiom. But the way it was said now by Kan gave it a more personal intonation.

On the way home she explained that she had become separated from Toby, without acknowledging why; and how she had been lucky enough to contact Clark at the hotel. When they got home, Kan repeated it in rapid Japanese to his father. Valerie thought Dr Tanaka did not look pleased, but his manners were much too good to allow him to utter one complaint at the alarm she had caused.

Next day it was lessons as usual. Valerie was working on *nageire* or tall vase styles, which required more deftness than the shallow-bowl arrangements because there was no pin-holder to keep the stems at the required angle. As the table next to her now, in place of Michiko, there was a little housewife who always wore a kimono in some shade of brown: tobacco brown one day, toffee brown another—a sad deputy for the bright-coloured Western dresses that Michiko wore. Neither was she as good at Ikebana as Michiko had been; she would often sit back on her heels and watch with envy as Valerie worked.

'Very good arrangement,' she said in halting English. 'Mimosa hard to trim. You have good hand.'

'Thank you,' Valerie said, pleased but knowing she must be modest, 'I think I've just been lucky today.'

'No,' said Dr Tanaka from behind her, 'it is not luck, Valerie. You have great talent. You do not use the flowers the way a Japanese girl would do, but the effect is always good.'

'Thank you,' she said, genuinely overwhelmed. Dr Tanaka almost never gave open praise.

'Perhaps,' he said thoughtfully, 'perhaps you do

not need any more lessons from us.' With another frowning glance at her arrangement and a little bow, he walked away.

She was startled. Not need any more lessons? It was nonsense! Why, she had only just started to get the feel of *nageire* balance, and there were all sorts of techniques for wedging or fixing the stems that she had not been taught, not to mention the nineteenth-century styles such as Ohara and all the other variations. Valerie had no illusions about her own ability; she had innate talent and was an unwearying worker, but she knew it might take years before she could produce Ikebana that reflected the glory of the old Japanese Flower Masters. She couldn't imagine what had prompted Dr Tanaka to speak like that. He must know as well as she did that she was only a beginner.

Toby rang, but she asked the maid to say she wasn't available. She felt sure he wanted to ask her out for the evening and she had no desire to go: after last night's extraordinary scene she preferred not to give him any reason to think he had claims on her. When Kan suggested they should go out for a walk in the mild April evening, she also refused. She wasn't quite sure why—perhaps she felt a quiet evening at home would be no bad thing.

The light was still good out of doors, so she took out her sketchbook to tidy up and fill in her rough notes on some of her class work. She had outlines of all the demonstrations and shorthand notes of the materials; she wanted to fill in some details in the sketches while her memory of the flowers was still vivid.

She was working away with coloured pencils, sitting on a stone bench at the edge of a little mossy incline, when Kan came out, carrying books.

'Mind if I share your bench?'

'Help yourself.'

'Let's see what you're doing. Say, that's pretty! That's a "boat at anchor" design, isn't it?'

'Kan, haven't you any work to do? I'll never get on if you talk to me.'

He made a face at her. 'All right, I'll read "King Lear"! A very Japanese-type piece of Shakespeare. Have you ever seen it, Valerie?'

'No, never. I will some day.'

'You like Shakespeare?'

'Kan, I'm trying to concentrate!' She felt about for her pencils. 'You've put your books on my pencils, you dreadful man! Now all the points are broken.'

'All right, all right, don't be cross with Kan, and Kan will sharpen all your pencils again for you.' He took a knife from his pocket, gathered up all the pencils, and set to work. But as he finished each one he insisted on testing the point by drawing in a few details on her sketches, and these he wickedly finished with little faces so that Valerie found herself with a brown chrysanthemum looking like a little rough-haired terrier, an iris like an elephant's head, and a carnation like a coy *geisha*. The sketches were talented and witty. Soon Valerie was giggling

83

over them and offering him a page of her sketchbook
to try something bigger.

The light began to go. There was a moth-like
fluttering on the path; Mrs Tanaka, wearing a
kimono as she sometimes did in the evening, had
come to shoo them indoors. ' It becomes damp,'
she explained.

' Did you read " King Lear ", my son?' inquired
Kan's father.

' No, sir, Valerie and I were talking.'

' I thought there was too much laughter to suit
a Shakespearean tragedy,' his father said.

The television was switched on; Dr Tanaka wanted
to see a programme about Hokaido, and his wife
obediently settled beside him on the sofa with her
embroidery. Kan was clearly not much interested;
he kept talking across the commentary to Valerie
until at last his father addressed a short command
in Japanese. After that he was silent, but sat watching Valerie as she went on with her class notes.

In the end, sensing that she was disturbing Dr
Tanaka, she went to her own room. She did the
work she had in mind to do, and then put away
her pencils. Before putting away her book, she
flipped the pages forward, to look at the sketch Kan
had done.

It was herself, seen as a Japanese would see her,
all flying blonde hair and angular limbs. She was
crossing the bridge at the foot of the hill, having
just come under the vermillion gateway, and was
carrying a vase of flowers in one hand and a map

of Kyoto in the other.

The whole thing was executed with so much insight and affection that Valerie smiled as she closed the book. But later, as she lay in bed, she thought about it again, with less amusement and more anxiety.

Since Michiko went away, Kan had given up all his spare time to Valerie. When he thought she had got lost in Kyoto's centre, he had come rushing out to fetch her home. Instead of studying, he teased her and laughed with her. And now the feelings betrayed by the sketch . . .

Could Kan be growing too fond of her?

Once the idea had occurred to her, more and more evidence seemed to support it: the uneasiness of his parents, the way they never left them alone together now, even strange remarks by Dr Tanaka that morning. 'Perhaps you do not need any more lessons from us.' Was it a half-expressed wish that she would go home?

For, of course, she quite understood that the Tanakas would not want their son to get mixed up with a Western girl. If they had thought Michiko unsuitable, how much more they would regret any involvement with Valerie!

But could it really be? Surely Kan wasn't so changeable as that. She hadn't been mistaken in thinking he cared for Michiko. He had been at the station, looking miserable the evening she left.

Yet all the same, if he had to give up Michiko because she hadn't the courage to stand up to parental disapproval, maybe he *would* turn to a girl like Valerie. Whatever else she lacked, Valerie wasn't short of the spirit of independence; the mere fact of having come here, to the other side of the world, to a land where she couldn't even speak or read the language, was a guarantee of her bravery.

The more she thought about it, the more the idea worried her. Could it be true? Did this account for the undercurrents she had felt in the Tanaka household?

And if it were true, what should she do?

She fell asleep at last, utterly incapable of deciding. Only one course of action had presented itself to her; she would ask Clark Cummings for his advice.

She rang him early next morning, before he would have had time to leave his hotel on business. He seemed surprised but pleased at her call.

'Could I speak to you some time, Clark?' she asked.

'How about now? I'm waiting to have breakfast brought in.'

'No, I can't, on the Tanakas' phone. Could I meet you somewhere?'

'Where, for instance? And when?'

'When is up to you. You've got business engagements. I could get away from class without much trouble if I wanted to.'

'How would it be if I bought you lunch? I've got an appointment at the Rukos' studio this morning, but I ought to be free by twelve-thirty. I'll

come to the campus and collect you so you won't
get lost!'

She told the Tanakas she would be lunching with
Clark. She noticed that they glanced at Kan on
hearing this; following their gaze, she saw a flicker
in Kan's eyes that might have been jealousy. She
waited rather anxiously to see what he would say,
but he had an English seminar today and would
not be back at lunchtime.

After morning class she walked down to the gateway. The fine weather had broken and a squally
rain was beating across the hill, rather like April
weather in England. She wore a poplin raincoat
in kingfisher blue which did double duty as a summer
coat, and a plain red silk headscarf.

Clark's car was already drawn up on the road
beyond the bridge. He opened the door as she ran
to avoid the rain; she tumbled in beside him.

'You look like one of those South African finches,'
he said. 'Rosy-crested something-or-others. It's
very fetching.'

'It's very wet,' she said, pulling off the scarf and
fluffing up her hair with the other hand. 'This will
knock the blossoms off the cherry-trees.'

'Oh, there's another lot just coming into bud,'
he said as they drove off. 'The Japanese have got
this thing organized, you know. As one variety gets
past its prime, another one is due to open. Then of
course there's the magnolia and the azalea and the
rhododendron—there are always trees in flower in
Japan, even in winter.'

87

She glanced at him. 'You really know an awful lot about Japan, don't you?'

'Only a fraction of what there is to know. But one can learn a lot simply by observation.'

They had turned, not back towards Kyoto as she had expected, but out to the north, towards open country. 'Where are we headed?'

'I thought you'd like to try something a bit different. There's a restaurant up on the road to Kamigamo Shrine where they catch their own fish and then cook it, fresh as last minute. There's a good view from the windows, too.'

He was quite right. They sat on cushions at a low table where the view of Higashiyama among the clouds was superb—just like the misty landscape to be seen on so many Japanese paintings. The food was as good as he had promised—about thirty little dishes brought in succession, each holding a different kind of fish or pickle or vegetable. Valerie used a fork, Clark used chopsticks as if he had grown up using them.'

'Now,' he said, 'tell me what's wrong.'

Now that she had to say it, she scarcely knew how to begin. It seemed a bit conceited to say, 'I think Kan Tanaka is falling in love with me.'

'The night before last,' she said at length, 'I had a quarrel with Toby.'

Clark paused with chopsticks over a dish of shrimp. 'Do you want me to carry a message to him? Because if you do, I'll have to refuse. I never meddle in the private affairs of my employees.'

He grinned. 'Sorry, that was pompous. Go on.'

'It's not about Toby. It's about what he said. He told me I was seeing too much of Kan, and said it would be wrong to imagine his parents approve of it. At the time I thought the idea was quite insane, but since then . . . Well, I thought I'd ask your advice.'

'Advice on what? On what Toby said?'

'No, on the situation at the Tanakas.'

'Is the situation there what Toby described?'

'Well, I . . .' She stammered into silence, then plunged on, rather pink in the face, to give the various little instances that she had recalled last night. 'What do you think?'

'M . . . mm,' Clark said. 'I must admit when he rushed to collect you at the Sakaki Hotel, I thought it was odd. I thought his parents would rely on me to bring you safely home, so I felt sure *they* hadn't sent him. And I must admit he and Toby glowered at each other as if they weren't the best of friends.'

'Then you think there might be something in it?'

'There might indeed. You're quite easy to get fond of you know, Valerie.'

She blushed and moved suddenly in embarrassment, upsetting one of the dishes of vegetables and bringing the little waitress scurrying to tidy up. When all was order again, she said manfully, 'But what about Michiko, Clark?'

'What about her? She's in Tokyo.'

'But he loves her.'

'So you say.'

'But he does, Clark! He was there at the station when she left, looking desperately unhappy.'

'All right, so he was in love with Michiko and maybe still is. What good does it do? She knows the whole idea is out of the question.'

He stopped. Valerie waited for him to go on.

'Aren't you going to protest that that's a cruel and monstrous thing to say?'

'No,' she sighed. 'I understand now that there can be a lot of pressure on a young couple in a situation like that. I rather expected Kan to follow Michiko, and since he didn't I suppose it means he's accepted the inevitable.'

'Exactly. Now you're beginning to understand the way things work. Kan and Michiko are obviously attracted to each other, but because she wouldn't defy the conventions, he's had to give up the idea. *That being so*, Valerie, I can quite see that Kan might fall in love with you. You have a lot of the qualities he probably saw in her—you're pretty and bright and good-natured. In addition you're not shackled with all the reverence for parental authority. So without thinking it through in any way, he lets you fill the gap in his life.'

'Oh dear,' she said. 'What will happen, do you suppose?'

'That depends on you.'

'On me?'

'On how you feel about Kan.'

'Oh! Well . . . I *like* him. Without him I think I might have found the Tanakas a bit too sedate. Kan is of this century—what Michiko calls "*modan*". He and I share a lot of interests.'

'But?' Clark prompted.

She spread her hands. 'I'm not the least bit in love with him.'

He nodded at her in approval, reached over and took one of her hands. 'Well said,' he remarked. 'I did have a suspicion that your romantic view of things might make you persuade yourself otherwise.'

'But what am I to do, Clark? If it was an English boy I could say, 'Look, it's all a mistake, let's cool it.'' But there's all this business of losing face—if I say a thing like that to Kan it will be a terrible blow.'

Clark laughed grimly. 'You're so right. Men have killed themselves in this country for less cause than that. No, no, you can't warn him off. But you can do something much more dignified and more final—you can remove yourself from the scene.'

'Remove myself?'

'Move out. Go and stay somewhere else till the course at the Ikebana school is over.'

Valerie was staggered at the thought. 'But where could I go?' she inquired. 'I can't afford a hotel. I could only come here in the first place because I was to be the Tanakas' guest.'

'You could stay with friends. That would be better, really. It would hurt the Tanakas' pride if you moved out to a hotel, but if you go to friends, it's easier.'

'But I don't *know* anyone in Kyoto.'

'You know me,' Clark said gravely.

Valerie stared at him, then saw the glint of mischief in his green-flecked eyes.

'Oh, you!' she said. 'I thought for a moment you were suggesting I should fly with you to the Casbah.'

'It would be a heck of a long flight. No, I could probably arrange for you to stay with some of the people I know. There're the Rukos—you've met them, but they don't speak much English. Then there's a lady I know who works in the Red Cross Hospital—she could probably put you up. She speaks English well, but she's often on night duty. Let's see—oh, there are a dozen or more. Give me a day or two to sort things out, and I'll see what I can do.'

'Clark, you really are kind,' she said.

'Come on, I'd better get you back to the school in time for the afternoon session. I've got to see accountants this afternoon to work out the cost of our new designs, so I mustn't be late. Off we go!'

As he set her down by the bridge, he said, 'I suppose . . . it would be a good thing, wouldn't it, if you could stay out of Kan's way. So how about coming out with me this evening?'

'Why, I'd love to, Clark.'

'Do you know,' he said, grinning, 'it will be the first time without Toby or Kan or the Misumi family?'

Laughing, she waved him goodbye.

But the laughter all died away when, as she came out of class that afternoon, a little Japanese messenger boy presented her with an envelope.

' Miss Stansgate? I know it is you—Cummings-*san* said the beautiful fair-hair lady! '

He ran off. She opened the letter and read:

Dear Valerie,

Wouldn't it just happen this way? The accountants tore apart the costing for the Rukos' new designs, so I have to go back to Toba Bay to see if I can buy something approximately the same only cheaper. Pearl-matching being what it is, I may be a day or two. Soon as I get back I'll fix up a place for you and we'll have that evening out. Yours, C.

Her heart sank. The idea of being delivered from the difficult situation at the Tanakas' had been so soothing. Never mind, it could only be another two or three days. She could manage to hold out until then.

That evening proved a difficult one. Kan chose to play his transistor radio rather loundly, while his father was dealing with some of the school's accounts.

Reproved for this, he switched it off and engaged Valerie in a conversation about life in England— the pop groups, the fashions, the freedom given to the young. The silence of his father grew more thunderous.

Valerie made as if to go to her room, but Mrs Tanaka made a little pleading gesture as if to say, ' Please stay.' Valerie realized that it was only her presence that prevented Dr Tanaka from venting his pent-up wrath on his son.

Next morning the household, as always, was astir early. But as Valerie came towards the breakfast room she realized the morning routine had been broken. The maids were scurrying about looking scared, and from inside the room Dr Tanaka's voice could be heard raised in an angry tirade.

Mrs Tanaka came out into the hall.

' What's wrong?' Valerie whispered.

Her hostess, white-faced, put her hands together in distress. ' It is Kan. He has been very foolish. This morning he asked his father to give him a bigger allowance because, he said, it was impossible to take a girl out and buy her European food on the small amount he gets.'

' Oh dear,' Valerie said. ' That wasn't very wise.'

' I don't know why he should do it. He must know his father is not pleased with him and so would not agree. I don't know,' said Mrs Tanaka, shaking her head anxiously, ' I don't know!'

Kan came stamping out of the breakfast room, pushed his shoes on his feet, and without a word to either of them went straight out and down the drive, walking fast. Every line of his back denoted mutiny.

His mother, after a glance at Valerie, folded her

hands before her and went in to speak to her husband. After a moment she reappeared.

' He wants to speak to you, Valerie.'

' Me?'

Mrs Tanaka nodded.

' Oh, very well.' Rather apprehensive, Valerie went into the breakfast room.

The sliding windows had been pushed open to let in the rain-washed air from the garden. Sunlight gilded all the little bowls and dishes on the breakfast table. Dr Tanaka sat by the window, his face grave but determined.

' Valerie-*san*,' he said, ' I think it would be better if you left my house at once.'

CHAPTER V

The silence in the room was intense after Dr Tanaka stopped speaking. Valerie stared at him mutely.

As the pause lengthened the doctor looked perturbed and cleared his throat. 'I have been very anxious for some time now,' he said. 'You must have seen that your presence here is very disturbing.'

'To . . . to Kan?' Valerie said.

'Ah, you don't pretend not to understand. Since your arrival I scarcely recognize my son. It is very important, Valerie, that Kan should have no distractions from his studies. Competition is keen at the examinations—even a few marks can make all the difference between success or failure. With you in this house I think his studies are being forgotten.'

Valerie could not find anything to say against this. She might have remarked that two or three weeks of inattention ought not to wreck Kan's university career, but she knew very well that wasn't the real problem. Dr Tanaka did not want to say outright: 'I think my son is falling in love with you and I want to prevent it,' but that was the basis of his anxiety.

'I was thinking of going anyhow,' she said. 'Perhaps to some friends.'

'Where? Tokyo?'

'No, here in Kyoto.'

Dr Tanaka looked away. 'I would prefer if you left Kyoto,' he said.

That shook Valerie. ' But . . . but my studies? I've only learned a quarter of—'

' I have friends among the other Flower Masters. I could arrange for you to continue your studies in Kobe, for instance.'

' Kobe? I know no one there. I don't even know where it is!'

' It is quite agreeable. I can telephone my colleague there and you can be on your way within an hour or two.'

Valerie felt a rising resentment. She could appreciate that Dr Tanaka was worried, but there was no reason to treat her like an exile.

' I have not the slightest intention of going to Kobe,' she said in a firm voice.

He gave her a stare of surprise. He was not accustomed to women uttering defiance.

' I think you had better do as I advise,' he replied, stern and paternal. ' After all, you have no one else to arrange things for you.'

' Good heavens, I don't *need* anyone! What do you take me for, a two-year-old? I shall go, since I agree it would be best, but I don't need any help from you except to call a taxi.'

' Very well,' he said, and clapped his hands. His wife—at attention outside the door and clearly aware of all that had been said—came hurrying in. He spoke to her in Japanese; she bowed and hurried out. A moment later Valerie heard her speaking on the telephone.

She glanced at Dr Tanaka. His face was

studiously impassive. As far as he was concerned the matter was closed. He had suggested she should go to a friend's house and she had chosen to go off on her own; to him it was a loss of face.

'Goodbye, Dr Tanaka,' she said, and left the room.

In her own room Mrs Tanaka was waiting. 'My dear,' she said—and it was the first time Valerie had heard her use a European endearment—'where will you go?'

'I'll go to the Sakaki Hotel. Toby-*san* is probably there, I'll talk things over with him.'

'Valerie, I am so sorry! I would do anything to help you, but my husband is head of the family . . .'

She was helping her to pack as they talked. She ascertained that Valerie had enough money for present needs and begged her to ring and ask for more if she needed it: 'Ring after nine in the morning tomorrow—my husband will be in the lecture hall then.'

Though she had no intention of doing any such thing, Valerie nodded and pressed her hand. The taxi had already arrived and was waiting by the bridge; the driver had come up to the house to carry her luggage.

She gave him her two cases and he went tramping off down the hill. Mrs Tanaka came to the door with her, her head turned away to hide her distress.

'*Sayonara*, Valerie-*san*. *Sayonara!*'

Defying Japanese convention, Valerie gave her a little hug and a kiss on the cheek. 'Goodbye, Mrs

Tanaka. I hope we meet again.'

On the drive to the hotel she reviewed the situation. She had a fair sum of money, having been allowed to spend almost nothing since her arrival. It would last three or four days if she could find some inexpensive hotel, but she could always cable her parents for more—though she would prefer not to do that. She had the return half of her air ticket home from Tokyo, so that was no problem.

At the Sakaki Hotel she had her luggage set down in the foyer. 'Bates-*san*?' she inquired.

The receptionist, a dapper young man, replied in English. 'Mr Bates has gone to Toba Bay with Mr Cummings. I understand they will be back two-three days.'

She hesitated. She'd known Clark was away, but had hoped to find Toby, who might have been able to suggest some course of action.

'Can I leave my luggage there while I have coffee?' she inquired, suddenly aware that she had come out without a bite to eat. 'And biscuits, please?'

'Surely, ma'am. In the lounge, that way.' He bowed and pointed. She went into the room where she had had tea the night she got lost.

She was drinking her coffee, and reflecting that in a hotel of this standing it would probably cost a fortune, when the swing doors burst open and Kan came hurrying in.

'Valerie! Are you all right?'

She sprang up to greet him. 'How did you know

99

I was here, Kan?'

'My mother told me. She's worried out of her mind about you. Valerie, what on earth happened?'

'Didn't she say? Your father asked me to leave.'

'But not like this!'—he gestured towards the vestibule where her luggage stood. 'Not at a moment's notice, surely?'

'He suggested I should go to a flower school in Kobe. I refused and walked out.'

'Oh, Val! Oh, good heavens! What can I say? It's archaic! It's so *like* my father—European top-dressing, Japanese bedrock!' He sat down beside her and took her hand. 'What are you thinking of doing now?'

'I really don't know. I came here because it was the only place I could think of, but both Clark and Toby are away.'

'Shall I get you a room here?'

'I couldn't possibly afford it, Kan. The prices are probably astronomical. Is there a YWCA here in Kyoto?'

'Yes, in Inagawa. I'll take you there.' He sat watching her as she fussed with the coffee-pot, then added, 'You're staying in Kyoto, then?'

'I don't know . . . I hadn't thought about it.' She did that now. 'Maybe it would make more sense to go to Tokyo? I shan't be going to the school here any more.'

'That's what I was thinking,' he said. 'How about this, Val—I take you to Tokyo to Michiko's house? She'll be happy to have you, and you wouldn't have to pay hotel or hostel fees.'

'Oh, would you, Kan? I must admit the idea of having to buy a train ticket to Tokyo was a bit intimidating.'

'Come on, then! The Tokyo Express leaves in a few minutes!'

'But what about your car?' she put in as he hustled her to the door.

'It is my father's car,' he said with hauteur. 'We leave *that* here.'

The Tokyo–Kyoto Express was a crack train, a streamlined, beautifully designed piece of modern technology. They climbed aboard with only minutes to spare.

'But, Kan,' Valerie said, getting her breath back, 'won't your mother be worried?'

'I'll call her from Tokyo.'

She sank back in her seat, her brain beginning to function at last. It was true that it seemed best for her to go back to Michiko's house in Tokyo, but for Kan too it had its attractions: he would see Michiko again!

'All right,' she said to herself. ' '' Journeys end in lovers' meetings,'' as they say.'

Still somewhat bewildered at the turn events had taken, but comforted at having Kan's companionship, she settled down to enjoy the train journey.

When she saw Mount Fuji again she knew they were close to Tokyo. She had had time to think now, and realized she should have left word for Clark at the hotel; he would be terribly worried when he rang the Tanakas and heard she was gone. When Kan rang his mother she must get him to ring the hotel also, to leave word.

They took a taxi from the station, Kan directing the driver with continual advice. At the gate of Michiko's home they drew up. Kan said, 'Here we are!', leapt out, and hurried up the path calling, '*Tadaima*, Misumi-*san*! Michiko-*san*!'

The door opened. Little Mrs Misumi appeared in kimono and frilled apron, her face a picture of complete astonishment. Kan paused, disappointed. He had forgotten Michiko would still be at work at this early hour of the afternoon, Valerie guessed—as had she herself.

They were invited in at once. Mrs Misumi fussed around bringing orangeade and sugar biscuits, too excited to attend to anything that Kan was trying to say. Finally she knelt on the *tatami* alongside, offering a dish of what looked like nougat; Kan took a piece, stayed her hand so that she remained attentive, and spoke seriously for a few minutes.

It was interesting to watch the expressions change on the little woman's face. First came surprise, then concern, then anxiety, and last of all a sort of subdued pleasure as she glanced from Kan to Valerie and back again. Kan ended with a question, to which Mrs Misumi replied fervently: '*Dozo, dozo.*' Which, Valerie remembered, seemed to mean something like 'Please do, please do.'

'Mrs Misumi says she would be delighted to have you stay here,' Kan explained. 'She's a bit surprised, of course, and I haven't bothered to give her all the details, but she's quite okay—no, I mean it's okay with her to have you here. Now if you'll excuse me, I'll go and fix myself up with a bed in a friend's house while you unpack.'

'You're staying?' Valerie commented, a bit surprised.

'Sure I'm staying. No point in going back to Kyoto while my father is in a bad temper. Give him a week or so and he'll have gotten over it. Okay if I leave you for now?'

'Yes . . . thank you,' she said.

He gave her a cheerful wave, bowed respectfully to Michiko's mother, and went.

Left with Mrs Misumi, Valerie found her difficulties just beginning. The little lady pushed her gently towards the room she had previously occupied, repeating ' *Dozo, dozo*,' so she took her cases in there. But then Mrs Misumi addressed a string of questions, none of which she could understand. Eventually, by mime, it was established that she was being asked if she was hungry and if she would like to wash; the answer to the first was a shake of the head and to the second ' *Dozo!* ' which made Mrs Mimusi laugh but had the desired result of being given the freedom of the bathroom.

Having bathed and changed, she felt much better. But to be candid it was not a comfortable situation; her hostess watched her with smiling attention, trying to anticipate her wishes—springing up to switch on the television, to offer cigarettes, to find maga-

zines (in Japanese, which Valerie couldn't read).
She tried to convey to Mrs Misumi that if there was
housework to be done, Mrs Misumi mustn't let
Valerie hinder her; and, indeed, that Valerie would
like to help. But this proved too complex, and in
the end they were reduced to a well-meaning silence.
She longed for Michiko to come home.

About half-past six there came the sound of light
footsteps on the path. The door stood open to the
warm evening air; Mrs Misumi darted to it chattering her news. Next moment Michiko was in the
room, petite and perfect as ever in a dress of rose-
pink cotton with a matching triangular headscarf.

'Valerie!' she exclaimed. 'How wonderful! I
didn't expect you for at least two more weeks. How
nice to see you!'

She bowed, but that was too formal for Valerie,
who threw herself upon her. 'Oh, Michiko, how
glad I am you're here! I've missed you. How
have you been?' She eyed her keenly. 'You look
a bit tired.'

'The day at the boutique seems long. We have
the new collection to sell. It is hard work. But
there—! She broke off. 'You are well? You,
also, look tired.'

'I'm quite well, thanks. A bit bothered.'

'Bothered?'

'It means . . . perturbed . . . worried.'

'Why are you worried, Valerie-*san*? Is anything
wrong?' And then, her mind moving quickly,
'You are here only for a day visit?'

'No, I . . . I'm staying for a while. Kan arranged it with your mother.'

'Kan?' Michiko turned at once, glancing into the other rooms. 'He is here?'

'He's been here. He brought me.'

'Brought you?'

'I'd better explain,' Valerie said with a sigh. 'Dr Tanaka asked me to leave. He had a dreadful quarrel with Kan this morning, and immediately after he called me in and asked me to go.'

Michiko's eyes widened. 'Asked . . . ? Why did he do this?'

'Because of the effect he said I had had on Kan. It was such a surprise—I mean, I know Kan and I had gone out quite a lot, but I shouldn't have said it amounted to . . . Well, anyhow, he asked me to leave, so I did.'

'And Kan came with you?'

'Yes. He's gone off to fix up a place to stay, but he said he would be back.'

Michiko sank down on the *tatami* in the kneeling position which seemed so natural and restful to Japanese women. She put her hands up to her cheeks. Then she spoke to her mother, obviously asking questions. Mrs Misumi shook her head, looked in wonder at Valerie, then half-smiled and shrugged.

After a moment Michiko said: 'We are honoured to have you here. Please stay as long as you wish.'

There was something rather formal about it. Valerie, who had hoped for a long, feminine discussion about what to do next, was a little chilled by her manner. Was it inconvenient to have her? Did they fear the expense of a house-guest?

'I should of course like to pay for—'

'Please!' Michiko said, holding up a small thin hand. 'That must not be talked of.'

Maybe it must not be talked of, but when she left for England Valerie intended to leave some useful but expensive present by way of a thank-you, or do something to show appreciation. She must ask Kan when he came.

She had intended to ask Michiko what she had better do about ringing the Sakaki Hotel and leaving a message for Clark or Toby, but somehow there seemed to be a restraint between them. She wondered if it was caused by anxiety on Michiko's part about how she and Kan would feel towards each other now: after all, last time they met they had been good friends, almost sweethearts, yet Michiko had withdrawn from the relationship out of respect (mistaken, Valerie thought) for their elders. What did she feel now?—regret, apprehension, eagerness, or simple embarrassment?

It seemed clear, from the open manner in which Michiko's mother had greeted Kan, that Michiko had confided none of her feelings. 'I suppose she wouldn't,' Valerie thought, 'if she felt her mother would disapprove.'

Dear me, what a mix-up it all was—like Victorian etiquette gone mad. Why couldn't people just behave naturally? Why did there have to be this exaggerated respect for older people, and those in authority, and rules that simply didn't fit in with the modern world?

Valerie caught herself up. She was beginning to think like Clark! It was he who had first said to her: 'The real Japan—you've no idea of it.' *This* was the real Japan—the simple everyday life in the Misumi household, where Mrs Misumi was not told by her daughter that there had nearly been a romance, where Michiko was perplexed over how to greet Kan when he came, and no one asked any impolite questions because it simply 'wasn't done'. It was all quite far removed from the grandeur of the Kabuki plays, the coy prettiness of the *geisha* dances, or the tranquillity of the great temple gardens.

A puzzling place.

When Kan arrived, only Valerie was near the little hall: Mrs Misumi and her daughter seemed to have disappeared as if by magic. Valerie said hello, then called, 'Michiko! Mrs Misumi! Kan's here.'

Mrs Misumi came hurrying, radiating goodwill. Michiko followed more slowly, looking down. Valerie had half hoped they would rush into each other's arms, but they did not: they stayed the requisite number of feet apart and exchanged bows of exquisite decorum.

'I give up!' thought Valerie. 'After being apart so long, they might at least show *some* emotion.' But no—from the way they acted it was impossible to judge what they were feeling. Certainly no one

would ever have guessed that this self-possessed
young man was the same as the one who had gazed
so longingly at the window of the train as Michiko
was borne away from Kyoto Station.

'Let's go out for a walk,' Valerie suggested. She
found the atmosphere in the Misumi household
rather stifling at present.

'Yes, we have to decide what to do,' Kan agreed.

'Did you find a place to stay?'

'No problem. The Yukinos are letting me use
their son's room—he's away at college. Ready to
go?'

'Yes, I'll just fetch a cardigan. Coming,
Michiko?'

Michiko drew back. 'No, thank you, I am rather
tired.'

'Oh, do come, the fresh air would do you good.'
'Silly girl,' Valerie was thinking, 'if I were as much
in love with Kan as you are, I'd go out for a walk
with him, and to blazes with what my parents said!'

But Michiko persisted in saying she was tired.
When this was translated for her mother's benefit,
she nodded, and made fluttering gestures implying
that Valerie and Kan should go out together. Sighing, Valerie looked at Kan, hoping he would add his
persuasions. But he remained silent and they at
last took their leave.

'Did you ring your mother?' Valerie inquired.

'Yes, I did.'

'Had she been worried?'

'Well, yes, I'm afraid so.'

'But you set her mind at rest.'

'Mm . . .' Kan said. 'I also rang the Sakaki Hotel and left a message for Clark. So everything is going according to plan.'

'I'd hardly say that,' she protested. '*I* haven't got a plan. I still really don't know what to do.'

'What do you *want* to do?'

'Well, I've been trying to think. I was wondering if it was worth while trying to get into another Flower School? There must be one in Tokyo.'

'Of course, several. But they all have a full complement of students, I should think. You might get into the Sogetsu, but that's a bit too advanced for you . . .'

Valerie shook her head. 'I think I'll just have to give up the idea of going on with Ikebana studies. Maybe I'd better just go home.'

'Oh, no, Valerie! Don't do that!'

To her surprise he took her hand and pressed it. It was such a rare gesture from him that it must betoken strong emotion. At her look of bewilderment he let go, then said, 'There's so much to see in Japan. Don't go back so soon. I'm staying in Tokyo at least a week—stay, and I'll take you to interesting places. You have not seen the iris gardens at the Meiji Shrine or been up Tokyo Tower —you can't leave Japan without seeing the view from Tokyo Tower!'

Despite herself, she began to laugh. 'My goodness, what a disaster it would be to miss the view from Tokyo Tower! Well, all right . . . What I think I'll do is this. Tomorrow I'll get you to take me to the Ikebana schools to see if anyone will take me for a few more lessons—I'd like to keep on until my money runs out, which will probably be quite soon if I have to pay high fees. In between classes I could see a bit more of Tokyo. And then I think that at about the end of another week I ought to fly home. What do you say?'

'Yes, that sounds very sensible.'

'Meanwhile I must send an air-letter to my parents to let them know my change of address. They'll think I'm still in Kyoto . . .'

It was a mild evening. They walked for a while round the Olympics Park, then took a subway back from Akasaka-Mitsuke. Kan parted from her at the door of the Misumis' house. 'I won't come in,' he said. 'Michiko is tired. Say goodnight to her for me. I've got to catch a streetcar to Meiji-Dori.'

Next morning, Valerie took care to stay out of the way in the little house until Michiko was ready to leave for work. They exchanged good-mornings, Valerie promised to call in at Michiko's shop and take her to lunch, and then Michiko hurried away, still curiously pale and silent.

Valerie washed and dressed. Since the day promised to be mild and sunny, she put on a navy linen skirt and a sleeveless white sweater, and was just trying the effect of a red-and-white striped scarf at the neck when she heard a well-known voice call: 'Tadaima! Misumi-san!'

'Clark!' she cried, running to the hall to meet

him. 'You got Kan's message then?'

'I got *a* message,' he replied, stooping to come in at the low doorway. He seized her by the shoulders. 'How are you? Are you all right? What on earth's been happening?'

'Oh, it was all so silly,' she said, and explained, as undramatically as she could, her departure from the Tanaka household. 'Then, you see, I didn't know what to do, so I went to the Sakaki Hotel, half hoping to find you or Toby. Kan caught up with me there and brought me to Tokyo.'

'Kan brought you?' he said, in almost the same tone as Michiko had said, 'Kan came with you?'

'Yes, he'll be calling for me soon.'

'He's here in Tokyo?'

'Yes, he thought he'd stay here until his father cooled down a bit.'

Clark ran a hand through his thick brown hair. His face was a study. 'He'll have a long wait,' he said. 'Valerie, have you *any* idea what you've done?'

'I've . . . come to Tokyo. Because I couldn't find anywhere to stay in Kyoto.'

'Lord above, why couldn't you have booked a room at the Sakaki?'

'I didn't have the sort of money that that would have cost,' she replied, beginning to get annoyed.

'Oh, you must surely have known that I'd lend you the money, and welcome! But no, you have to come rushing off to Tokyo with handsome young Kan Tanaka. Do you know what such behaviour means to a Japanese?'

'No,' said Valerie faintly. But she was beginning to have an inkling.

'In the eyes of every Japanese—Kan included, I've no doubt—it's an elopement. Everybody expects you and Kan to get married now.'

CHAPTER VI

Valerie felt herself go hot and then cold at Clark's words.

Elope with Kan? Nothing could have been further from her mind. She had removed herself from his father's house without too much protest (though with some stifled resentment) simply because she wanted to be less involved in Kan's life.

'M-married?' she stammered. 'But I don't want to marry Kan!'

'Then why the dickens did you come away with him? It was a crazy thing to do!'

'But . . . but . . . you said yourself, Clark, it would be a good thing to get away from the Tanakas' house—'

'But not with Kan Tanaka as your runaway companion. For Pete's sake, Valerie, haven't you any sense? Have you learned nothing since you've been here?'

Valerie's reply to this was astounding. To her own amazement and dismay, she burst into tears.

'Don't . . . oh, don't . . . I can't bear it if you're a-angry, Clark!' she sobbed. 'Please . . . !'

Her vision was blurred. She felt behind and around her for a chair to sink into, quite forgetting that there were none in the room. Her hand came into contact with the front of Clark's lightweight worsted jacket. An arm came round her. She laid her head against a solid, comforting chest, and wept unashamedly.

Clark was saying soothing things. 'Don't, now, ah, don't. Poor little love. Was I a brute? I'm sorry, darling. Mop your pretty eyes. There, there.'

It was so consoling, so delicious. She would have liked to hear his voice croon on for ever on that note of gentle solicitude.

But in this world moments of exquisite pleasure are shortlived. In a Japanese dwelling as small as the Misumis', sounds could be heard across two or three rooms' breadth. Mrs Misumi came bustling in, all solicitude, uttering cries of startled interrogation.

Without letting go of Valerie, Clark made brief replies. He sent Mrs Misumi off for first aid measures, which appeared in the form of a small cup of saké. Clark made her sip it. She made a face and tried to avoid the rest.

'Drink it,' he insisted. 'Come on, now, down it goes. Swallow it.'

Like a child taking nasty medicine, she submitted. In the meantime, Clark was giving instructions to Mrs Misumi. One of the low tables was brought forward and covered with cushions, so that a place was made for Valerie to sit in comfort until she recovered. He crouched at her side, dabbing at her cheeks with his handkerchief.

'There now. Better?'

She nodded. Mrs Misumi took the saké cup from

her, uttering little chirruping sounds. Valerie produced a wavering smile for her.

'People don't really think I'm going to marry Kan?' she said.

'They certainly do. I rang Mrs Tanaka before I left Kyoto, and she takes it for granted you'll come back as her daughter-in-law.'

'Is she very upset?'

'Well . . . yes. I think she could accept it herself, but her husband is furious about the whole thing, so naturally Mrs Tanaka is very distressed. It sounded as if the doctor had said he would never speak to Kan again.'

'Great heavens, what a mess!'

'I take it you didn't expect to end up with a wedding ring when you left Kyoto.'

'No, of course not.'

'You don't love Kan?'

'No.'

'Have you ever given him any reason to suppose you love him or want to marry him?'

'Oh, Clark!' Her tone of protest was answer enough.

'But being in love with you, he thought he had reason to believe you love him. What's that bit in Shakespeare . . . "trifles light as air are to the jealous confirmations strong as proofs of holy writ".'

'Clark, I swear to you I never said or did anything to lead Kan on to believe I loved him. We never kissed, we never even held hands. Why, I even thought that he came with me to Tokyo simply to see Michiko.' At the name Valerie put her hand up to her mouth in dismay. 'Michiko! Does *she* believe I'm going to marry Kan?'

'Undoubtedly.'

'Oh, how dreadful, how absolutely *dreadful*! No wonder her manner to me has been so cool and strained. And I hadn't any idea . . . !' Valerie clutched at Clark. 'She can't really believe I'd come here and claim hospitality if Kan and I—? Oh, Clark, you must be wrong.'

'We'll soon find out,' he said grimly. He turned to Michiko's mother and had a rapid conversation, during which she nodded vigorously several times and gave sideways glances at Valerie. Finally Clark explained, 'Mrs Misumi was asked by Kan to take you in for a while because you had had to leave his father's house due to his father's hostility to you. She took this to mean "hostility to your marriage", for anyhow you wouldn't travel alone from the house of a guardian (meaning Dr Tanaka) with a young man *unless* you intended to marry him.'

'And Michiko?'

'When Michiko came home, Mrs Misumi told her you were here to stay until you and Kan got married. Kan said nothing that dispelled this idea, I gather.'

'I don't understand it,' Valerie burst out. 'Kan isn't an idiot. He must know as well as you do that a European girl doesn't think she's going to marry a man, just because they took a train journey together! He *must* know I'm not thinking of marrying him.'

'I don't know so much—'

'Clark, believe me. You know more about Japanese manners than I do, but I know more about Kan. He speaks English absolutely fluently, he reads English books—'

'Shakespeare and Milton,' Clark suggested.

'No, no, American magazines and newspapers, too. He *knows* that before an English girl gets married, she discusses the idea with the man—she isn't informed by her parents or picked out by a marriage-broker! Kan Tanaka doesn't for one minute think I'm going to marry him.'

Clark studied her with dispassionate interest. 'You speak with certainty. I'm inclined to believe you. So the question now is—why has Kan led you into this very compromising situation?'

'Led me?'

'Of course, led you. He knew, if you didn't, what people would expect after this runaway trip. He knew his father would take it for granted you were getting married. He knew Mrs Misumi and her daughter would think the same.'

'I don't understand it,' Valerie mumbled.

'I think maybe I do. Young Kan Tanaka thought he could pressure you into marrying him because it would be the expected thing.'

'Oh, no, Clark—'

'Oh, yes, Valerie. I'm going to have a word

117

with that young man! Where does he hang out?'

'He's staying with a friend—Yukino, I think the name was.'

'Any idea what address?'

'He said he had to catch a streetcar to Meiji-Dori.'

'Ah. That's easy, then—the police patrol will have the family's house on their map. Come on, then—pack up your things.'

She rose, but hesitated. 'Where am I going, Clark?' she said in a low, distressed voice.

'Well, you can't stay here, can you? Not in the house of the girl who fell in love with Kan herself. It would hardly be kind, would it?'

'No, I suppose not.' She hung her head, not daring to look at him.

'So the best thing is for you to come to my hotel. No—' he held up a hand as she opened her mouth— 'don't say you can't afford it. I'll pay for the room and you can pay me back some day. Off you go and get ready.'

He was already explaining to Mrs Misumi before she could utter another word. Secretly glad to have the situation taken out of her hands, Valerie went to stow her nightdress and cosmetics back in her case.

Clearly somewhat puzzled, Mrs Misumi bowed them out. 'I simply told her we felt you'd be more comfortable at a hotel,' Clark said as he helped Valerie into the Honda. 'This whole thing is going to be dreadfully hurtful to the dignity of the Tanaka family, so the less we discuss it, the better.'

Valerie nodded in agreement. She didn't want to talk about it to anyone. It was all a dreadful mix-up, and she was sorely tempted to take the first flight home to England just so as to avoid all the unpleasantness that must surely follow.

The Azia Hotel was bustling with life as they drew up, although it was still only the breakfast hour. Businessmen of all nationalities were meeting and greeting each other while tourists, mainly American, pored over the coach-tour timetables.

It wasn't quite so easy to get a room as Clark had implied. The reception clerk looked dubious. ' We have nothing available, Mr Clark. The hotel very occupied. We have Japan Air Lines group-tour staying here two night, so all rooms booked.'

' Oh, come on, Noburu, you must have a corner somewhere for this little lady. She's got nowhere to go.'

' Very sorry. In two days' time, Mr Clark, several rooms vacant.'

' Be a pal, Noburu—'

' Look, Clark,' Valerie put in, ' I can go somewhere else for two nights.'

' I don't think so,' said Noburu, shaking his sleek dark head. ' Hotel very difficult for European just now—special Kabuki Festival is on, and special exhibition of art treasures at Ueno Park attracts many visitors. Plenty hotel for Japanese travellers but not so easy European.'

' Then that's easy,' Clark said. ' You'll have my room and I'll move out for a couple of days—'

'No, no, I wouldn't dream of it! *I'll* go to a Japanese hotel—'

'To the *ryokan*? You can't speak the language —how could you manage? I'll be all right in a *ryokan*.'

'But you don't like Japanese food—'

'I'll survive,' he said. 'Okay, then, Noburu. This is Miss Stansgate. She'll have my room until another one becomes available. Here, boy!' He beckoned to a page, gave him Valerie's cases, and took the key from the reception clerk.

His room was on the first floor, a very pleasant one with three pale yellow walls and one consisting entirely of windows, shaded now by reed screens on which were painted landscape scenes. There were two flower arrangements, one a European fan-shape on a low table, the other an Ikebana on a shelf. Valerie's practised eye established at once that the Ikebana was not as good as those she could produce. Besides the flowers, there was a television, a radio, a telephone, a tape-recorder and a record-player, all neatly set into a special fitment alongside a desk where a typewriter stood.

'Good gracious, is all that stuff yours?' Valerie gasped.

'No, no, only the tape-recorder and the typewriter. The rest is all standard equipment in the hotel. Look, have a look around while I throw a few things into a case.'

'Clark, I feel awful about pushing you out—'

'Nonsense, nonsense, I'm used to being on the

move. I've got suits of clothes hanging in hotel rooms in Tokyo, Kyoto, Toba, and Osaka. One more move won't hurt me.' As he spoke Clark was putting shirts into a zip bag, collecting shaving-tackle from the bathroom. 'There now. You make yourself at home. I'm off to check in at a *ryokan* and then find our young friend Kan Tanaka. And when I do,' he added with a growl in his voice, 'I'll probably wring his confounded neck!'

As he was closing the door Valerie called, panic-stricken, 'Clark!'

'What?'

'When shall I see you again?'

'Couple of hours, I'd say.'

'What shall I do until then?'

'Have breakfast—what else?' he grinned, and was gone.

When she had unpacked a few things and tried all the knobs on the radio and television, Valerie became aware she was hungry: once again she'd taken a hasty departure without eating breakfast. She went down to the dining-room, was relieved to find a menu printed in English, and ordered 'The American Breakfast of orange juice, scrambled eggs, and coffee. The waiter brought her an English language newspaper. She settled down to the luxury of a meal in a first class hotel.

But at the end of an hour she had finished the paper and emptied the coffee pot. She strolled through the public rooms of the Azia, admiring the modern décor and the comfort. She read the brochures in the hotel lobby. And still it was only eleven o'clock.

She sat down in the lounge, her mind going over the situation. Clark had said it would be wise not to discuss it with anyone and had therefore left Mrs Misumi in the dark about the supposed marriage of Kan and Valerie.

But surely poor Michiko deserved to know the truth?

The more she thought about it, the more Valerie wanted to clear things up with Michiko. It was true that nothing she could say would bring Kan within Michiko's reach, but at least it would be a comfort to her to know that Valerie had no intention of marrying him.

She had promised this morning to take Michiko to lunch. She would do that now.

She asked the reception clerk to look up Michiko's shop in the trade directory; it was called Iris Boutique. When he had found it, he marked it on a street plan of Tokyo Centre.

' If Mr Clark comes back before I do, will you tell him this is where I've gone?' she said.

She went out into the mild, cloudy morning. The crowds in the street were moving briskly, the girls in light Western dresses or cotton kimonos, the men mostly in sober suits. She passed the Ginza Church and then the great department stores—Hankyu, Mitsukoshi, Mitsukaya; then she came to the turning in which, according to the hotel clerk, she would find the Iris Boutique. She glanced at her watch; a little after twelve noon. Perhaps a little early for lunch, but Michiko might like to go for a stroll.

The shop had an avant-garde exterior and only one model dress on show in the circular window—clearly it was an expensive place. She went in, wondering if she could take off her shoes in a Japanese shop, but the young lady drifting towards her was wearing black patent court shoes, so that was all right.

'Misumi-*san*?' she asked.

The assistant smiled and nodded. A moment later Michiko came to greet her, together with the manager of the shop, his assistant manager, and three salesgirls. They were quite enthralled with Valerie's fair hair, prompting Michiko to ask on their behalf if it was washed every day to keep it so bright and did she darken her brows or were they naturally more brown than her hair?

It was clear that Michiko's prestige was increased by having such an unusual and interesting friend. Valerie was conducted to the manager's office, the inevitable tea was brought, and minutes flew past with time-consuming politeness.

At last, all smiles, the manager bowed them out. It was implied that Michiko could take as long as she liked for lunch. In great relief, Valerie hurried her out.

They walked towards Hibiya Park, next to the Imperial Palace. There they found a park bench. Valerie pulled Michiko down beside her, and spoke earnestly.

'Michiko, forgive me.'

'Forgive? For what?'

'For being so insensitive and so ignorant. Clark came to your mother's house this morning and explained how it must look to you. Until he pointed it out, I had no idea you would think I . . . I . . .'

Michiko remained silent, refusing to help her out of her embarrassment. Valerie plunged on.

'Michiko, I am not in love with Kan. I am not going to marry Kan.'

The Japanese girl looked up, startled into staring full at her, her black eyes wide with surprise.

'But he brought you—'

'He didn't. I *came* to Tokyo, and he came with me.'

'And you feel nothing to him?'

'*For* him,' Valerie corrected. 'Well, of course I feel something for him—comradeship, sympathy, gratitude. But I have no intention of getting married to him.'

Michiko looked down at her hands. 'Kan has intention,' she murmured.

'No, Michiko.'

Michiko nodded her head in stubborn affirmation. 'He must wish it,' she said. 'He would not have come away with you like runaway lovers, except—'

'Oh, please do stop talking like something out of a Kabuki play!' Valerie exclaimed; and then, appalled at her own rudeness: 'No, I'm sorry, I shouldn't have said that. But do see sense, Michiko love. We *aren't* like runaway lovers. His father asked me to go. I got cross and walked out at once.

Kan got worried—and that was kind of him, but really it's what any decent young man would feel. After all, Michiko, I can't speak the language, I don't understand the money, I couldn't even get on a train and be sure of getting off at the right station. I'd think poorly of Kan if he hadn't come after me. But it was nothing to do with runaway love.'

Michiko ran a finger along a crack in the park bench. 'In your country it would not mean love?'

'In *this* country it doesn't mean love,' Valerie replied. 'I swear to you I'm not in love with Kan.'

'Ah,' Michiko said, her voice full of tears, 'but do you swear Kan is not in love with you?'

Valerie searched her mind for an answer, but nothing came. She wanted to speak with conviction but could not. She didn't understand Kan's attitude, couldn't explain it.

Michiko spoke gently. 'You are very good, Valerie, very honourable and honest. You speak to me openly because you know I have deep feeling for Kan, though I try not. I am grateful to you—you want to make me happier because you are not taking Kan. But, Valerie—' she sighed—'you cannot take what I do not have. Kan does not belong to me. One day he will marry someone—I must accept this.'

Valerie would have liked to gainsay this, yet her intelligence told her Michiko was right. 'Well, anyway,' she said lamely, 'it won't be *me* that marries him. You and I have nothing to begrudge each other.'

' Begrudge?'

' It means want to take away from each other. Oh, Michiko, I only wish there was something I could do for you . . .'

' There is nothing, thank you. I think now that I should have done this thing for myself. If I had shown Kan that I would be *modan*, he might have spoken to his parents about me. But I was not brave enough and came home obediently to my mother . . . So perhaps Kan decided a girl from the real *modan* world would be better. And perhaps he is right.'

Valerie shook her head. ' It doesn't make sense, Michiko. He can't seriously think I . . . Oh well, never mind. Let's go and have something to eat.' She jumped up, pulling the other girl with her, and together they wandered under the trees in Hibiya until they came to an avenue with shops and restaurants.

Over lunch she explained to Michiko that she had gone to stay at the Azia Hotel. ' Clark is paying for the room, so of course I can't stay long. I've decided to send an airmail to my family saying I'm cutting short my visit, just to prepare them, and then I'll fly home at the weekend.'

' Two more days?' Michiko said. ' Stay longer, Valerie.'

' I don't think I'd better, Michiko. My money wouldn't last out.'

' Come back and stay with my mother. Much cheaper than Azia Hotel,' Michiko said, smiling.

'No, thanks all the same. It's all too awkward and complicated. If Kan came visiting me at your mother's house, I'd feel awful about it.'

Michiko couldn't deny that this would be painful to her, so she let her protest die. 'But still I am sorry if you go,' she said. 'Your holiday is spoiled because of me and Kan.'

And as this was, alas, only too true, they talked of something else.

After lunch they spent an hour in one of the big department stores, which was very like those in the shopping centres of Manchester or London. Valerie then accompanied Michiko back to the Iris Boutique and took a streetcar back to the Azia.

Once there she discovered she was very weary. The dramas of the last two days had taken their toll, she had had a restless night on the sleeping mats at Mrs Misumi's, and today she had walked miles. She decided to write to her mother, then have a bath and take a nap. When she collected her room key the desk clerk gave her a note: 'Mr Cummings called. He has been unable to contact Kan so far, but hopes to see him soon. He will be back by and by.'

In her room she rang for service and ordered English tea with milk and sugar. While she drank it she wrote her letter, glossing over her departure from Kyoto by saying the Tanakas had domestic troubles. She didn't want her parents to worry. She said that she would probably be home soon after they received her letter, that she was staying at the

Azia Hotel and was in no need of money because Clark, whom she had mentioned in previous letters, had once more come to her aid and could be repaid by and by.

That done, she proceeded to have a long and luxurious bath, after which she wrapped herself in one of her souvenir kimonos and lay down on the bed. As she grew drowsy it occurred to her that it would be a good thing to get her letter in the post so that it would catch the night flight; she rang room service to ask for someone to take away her tea-tray and collect her letter.

She was more than half asleep when she heard the room door open. 'The waiter,' she told herself sleepily, making no effort to open her eyes.

There was no sound of the tray being moved. She pulled herself up on an elbow, calling: 'Clark? Is that you?'

But the door closed without reply. She snuggled down again and went fast asleep. When she woke someone had been in to clear the tray and take her letter, and it was close on six o'clock, time to get dressed for dinner.

In honour of her elegant surroundings, she dressed with care. She took out of her case an uncrushable dress of lilac silk jersey, never worn so far because social occasions on this trip had been fewer than she expected. She brushed her hair, applied a little skin freshener, made up her eyes, and on the whole was not displeased with the effect. She was perhaps a little thinner and paler than hitherto, but that was not surprising in view of the anxieties of the last few days. But the rest had done her good, and if the sparkle in her eyes now had something to do with the idea of seeing Clark soon, it did her no harm.

The phone rang. Answering it, she said: ' Stansgate-*san*.'

There was a laugh on the other end of the line. ' And this is Cummings-*san*. How are you?'

' I'm fine. How about you?'

' A bit ragged round the edges. Can I come up and talk to you? I've something interesting to tell you.'

' About Kan?'

' Yes.'

' Come on, then. I'm dying to hear.'

A few minutes later he knocked on the door. ' I asked them to bring us something to drink,' he said. ' I need something, I can tell you. I've been chasing Kan all day.'

' Come in, sit down.' She cleared her kimono from an armchair. ' What happened?'

' I tracked down his friend's house, the Yukino family. They said he'd gone out—to the Misumis. I dashed back there—Mrs Misumi told me he'd been there but left on hearing I'd whisked you off. Presumably he'd gone back to his friends, so I went there again. Eventually he turned up. That was about four o'clock this afternoon. He was relieved to see me—said he'd been trying all the hotels to find you.'

The waiter came with the drinks—sherry for Valerie and a large Japanese beer for Clark.

'So what happened?' she urged after he had quenched his thirst.

'We had a long talk. I asked him straight out if he realized what his family expected to happen, and he said "Yes, they think I am going to marry Valerie." So I said "And is that what you think?" —and guess what he said?'

'I daren't,' Valerie said. 'Go on.'

'He said, "Of course not."'

'What?'

'You may well say "What"!' Clark said, setting down his glass. 'I nearly blacked his eye for him.'

'But what was it all about, then?' Valerie demanded. 'If he knew how it would look to his parents, why did he do it?'

'He did it *because* it would look like that to his parents,' said Clark. 'He wants them to think he's marrying you.'

Valerie put a hand to her forehead. 'I'm not sure I understand that,' she said faintly.

'How could you? No one as straightforward as you would ever catch on to a devious game like that. Quite simply, Kan wants to give his parents one helluva fright, so that when they discover he hasn't married this totally unsuitable foreign girl they'll be so relieved that they won't mind a bit when he starts dating a nice Japanese girl like Michiko.'

There was a silence.

'Valerie?' Clark said. 'Don't be upset.'

'I'm not upset. It's just so . . . underhand.'

'Well, you know all's fair in love and war. Kan did what he thought was necessary.'

'Without telling me?'

Clark came over and took her hand. 'Poor Valerie. You're really shocked, aren't you? I wish you'd . . .'

'What?'

'Come to terms with the fact that Japan is *different*. Men in this country don't think of treating women as equals. Even Kan—a twentieth-century type if there ever was one—he doesn't dream of taking either you or Michiko into his confidence. He simply worked out a plan and went ahead with it.'

'Using me as a sort of pawn.'

'I'm afraid so.' He picked up her sherry glass and refilled it. 'Drink this. You'll feel better.'

'No, thanks, I'm all right. I'm just . . . I think I'm angry.'

Clark rubbed his chin. 'I suppose you've a right to be. It certainly isn't a pleasant thought, to feel you've been made use of. But if you could bring yourself to feel kindly towards Kan, he'd like to say he's sorry.'

'Is that the message he sent?'

'Yes. He'd like to come himself and say so. I said I'd ring him.'

'I don't want to see him,' Valerie said. She was shaking with anger.

Clark shrugged. 'That's up to you, of course. I think he's genuinely sorry—'

'Sorry? What's he got to be sorry about? According to you he's quite sure what he did was justified.'

'Well, yes, but then you see you've got to accept that—'

'Accept? I don't have to accept anything. *I'm* not going to be treated like a second-class citizen by Kan or anyone else. Being a man, you wouldn't understand how humiliating it is to—'

'Now wait a minute, Valerie. There's no need to take that tone. I'm only saying that Kan's point of view is perfectly valid, in the context of his own society. The fact that he wants to apologize to you is a token of how much he likes you.'

'Likes me! In the same way you'd like a kitten or a budgie!'

'It's not me that—'

'But you condone it! You condone his behaviour.'

'I don't condone it. I accept it.'

'Well, I don't. And I shan't see him.'

'Well, that's beaut,' Clark said in exasperation. 'I spend the whole confounded day running round trying to find him—'

'No one asked you to,' she flared.

'But you wanted this business cleared up, didn't you? Or did you?' he broke in on himself. 'Did you want to go on believing Kan was mad about you? Is that what's at the bottom of this fit of pique

—sheer injured vanity?'

She sprang up, her cheeks hot, her mouth dry. 'How dare you! Who gave you the right to speak to me like that?'

'Oh, talking's no use! You're barricaded in behind your own prejudices. Only a good shaking would make any difference.'

'And you think you're the one to give it?' she inquired dangerously.

As soon as she had issued the challenge she knew it was a mistake. Weary and frustrated as he was, he rose to it at once. He seized her by the shoulders and for one moment, as his fingers gouged into the shield of flesh along the bone, she thought he was going to shake her hard.

But in the next moment he had pulled her roughly towards him, so that his arms came about her. She felt the tightening of his muscles; she was held fast, and close against him. A momentary glimpse of his face—angry, almost fierce, and yet full of longing.

His mouth was on hers. There was a silken strength in the kiss that momentarily overpowered her senses. She felt an indolent fire run through her veins.

But then anger, indignation, resentment, contempt—all these raced to her defence. She pulled back, struggled.

At first he would not let her go. When he did, perhaps her unwillingness was not the cause. It was something more mundane—someone was knocking on the door.

133

A moment later it swung open.

'Toby!' she cried, engulfed in relief. Toby's presence would protect her.

'Hello,' he said. 'Did I . . . interrupt something?' He was glancing from her to Clark, and back again.

Clark had drawn away. His face was hard and shuttered.

'Come in,' Valerie said. She had difficulty controlling her voice. 'I didn't know you were in Tokyo?'

'Got back from Toba Bay this afternoon,' he explained. 'I didn't expect to find *you* here, Valerie.'

'No . . . well, I had to leave Kyoto . . .'

'I'm sorry if I'm in the way,' Toby said. 'There was a difficulty over the contract that I wanted to discuss, Clark.'

'It can wait,' said Clark. He walked to the door. 'Come on,' he said to Toby.

With a grimace of bewilderment, Toby followed him.

Valerie sank down on the edge of the bed, shaken and trembling. No one had ever treated her like that before; no one had ever spoken to her like that. She would never speak to him again as long as she lived!

For some minutes her dazed mind refused to register anything further. But after a time her thought processes took over.

She couldn't stay here now. She couldn't be

beholden to a man like that for anything. She would pack her things and get out—now, at once! She swung her case on to the bed and began haphazardly to cram in the few belongings she had unpacked, snapped the locks shut, and then stood for a moment, trying to think.

There was nowhere else to go now but home— home to England. In the space of forty-eight hours she had lost all the friends she had made in Japan. How could it have happened? Where had she gone wrong?

Well, it didn't matter any more. She would ask the hotel's information service for the time of the next flight to London, take a taxi to the airport, and arrow home to people she understood and could trust.

She picked up the phone. The desk clerk said there was a London-bound flight at ten-ten p.m. She thought about that for a moment, and decided it was still too early to leave for the airport. She would have a meal first. She asked for a porter to take her luggage down and left her cases by the door.

Downstairs dinner was being served. She walked indifferently into the restaurant, thinking only that it would help to pass the time and scarcely aware of it when someone touched her on the arm.

'Valerie! Valerie, how nice! Are you dining alone?'

She turned slowly, to find Toby at her elbow.

'May I join you?' he asked.

'Why not?'

The waiter was leading them to a quiet corner. They took their places; the menu was proffered. She stared at it unseeing. Toby said: 'Shall I order?' and took it from her.

'Now,' he said, when the waiter had gone, 'tell me what's going on.'

She studied him, scarcely seeing him, her mind occupied with an internal debate about the scene between herself and Clark. What had ever made him imagine that she would submit to treatment like that?

'. . . Could see something was wrong,' Toby was saying.

'What?'

'I said, the minute I walked in I could sense it. You looked as if the sky had fallen in on you.'

'Yes . . . I was upset.'

'Had a row?'

'Yes.'

'I must say I was . . . well, I was staggered. I never thought Clark was the type.'

'No.'

The waiter brought the first course—iced melon. Valerie picked up her fork, but the idea of actually swallowing food was too absurd.

'I don't really understand what you're doing here,' Toby prompted.

'Here . . . ? Oh, I told you. There was a bit of trouble, in Kyoto.'

'With Kan?'

'Yes.'

'I told you you were getting in too deep with him,' Toby said, with a kind of gentle triumph.

'You were right,' she said. 'I should have listened to you.'

'Poor Val,' Toby said, reaching out to touch her hand.

They were silent for a moment or two. Then Toby said, 'Eat your food, my angel.'

'I don't really want it.'

'But you need it. You look exhausted.'

'No, I'm quite all right. I'm not really tired—I slept this afternoon.'

He flashed her a strange glance, but she was paying so little attention that she saw nothing in it.

'So what it amounts to is that you're pretty disillusioned with both Kan and Clark.'

'You could say so,' she answered bitterly.

'But you've still got me, Valerie.'

As if the curtain had gone up at a theatre to reveal Toby alone upon a stage, she was all at once aware of him. A moment ago he had had almost no existence; now here he was, sitting across from her, looking concerned.

'Oh, Toby,' she said with a catch in her voice. 'And last time we had dinner together I was absolutely horrible to you!'

'Never mind that now,' he said, pressing her hand. 'The only thing I regret about that evening is that I couldn't get my warning across to you. I got too emotional, and you quite rightly walked out on me.'

'I'm sorry, Toby. One of my troubles has always been that I act too impulsively.'

Toby smiled so that his honey-brown eyes lit with a sparkling warmth. 'I'd rather have that than a girl like Michiko,' he said, 'who seems to have no will of her own.'

'But that's because of her upbringing. Clark says—' She broke off.

He waited until she looked up and met his gaze. 'I could have told you about Clark, too,' he said. 'If I'd been around to see what was happening, I'd have warned you that he gives nothing for nothing. A business type—I've been working with him for nearly three months now and I can tell you this: I wouldn't like to be the fly in the web of *that* spider!'

'And yet,' Valerie protested, 'I've seen him do so many kind things . . .'

'Window-dressing! All part of the image. Look how he butters up the people here—learn the language, bow to this man, bow to that—and yet you know as well as I do he despises them.'

'Oh, I don't think he—'

'Of course he does! He won't eat their food or look at their paintings or bother with their history. All he does is put on a show of courtesy, but underneath he's thinking how to make money out of it. Why, remember what he said about that centuries-old headdress for the Goddess of Mercy—" Twenty thousand pearls in it "—he could probably have told you how much it would cost to break it up into costume jewellery.'

It was true. She remembered how at the time his remark had jarred upon her.

'Well, let's forget about him,' she said with forced brightness. 'I shan't be seeing him again.'

'Isn't he coming back tonight?'

'I've no idea. If he does, I shan't be here. I'm taking the ten-ten flight back to England.'

Toby's face went blank with disappointment. 'Valerie!'

'Well, what's the point of staying? My Ikebana classes are washed out, I've nowhere to stay—'

'But what about Michiko?'

'No, I can't. I'd meet Kan there, and I couldn't bear it. No, honestly, there's no one in Tokyo who cares tuppence about me.'

'Except me,' he said. 'You knew I'd put that in, didn't you? You must know, Valerie, I think the world of you. After we had that silly disagreement I tried to put you out of my mind, but seeing you again today has made me realize how strongly you've taken hold of me.'

He was trying to hold her gaze, willing her to feel some of his emotion. She was reluctant to become too deeply moved by his words; she still felt oddly drained and empty. Luckily the waiter came at that moment to serve the next course, and the tension was broken.

When he had gone Toby said, 'You don't really have to go back tonight, Valerie.'

She nodded with stubborn determination. 'Yes, I've made up my mind. My bags are packed, ready to go.'

' You'd go and leave me, just when we've found each other again?'

' But, Toby . . .!' She paused, trying to summon her forces. ' Toby, I'm in such a muddle at the moment. This last couple of days I've been through one shock after another, I don't really know whether our meeting again has as much meaning for me as it has for you.'

' But if you go tonight, how are you ever going to find out?'

She sighed. She wished he wouldn't try to persuade her of something that seemed to her very unsure. Was there anything between herself and Toby? She liked him; he was good fun. He had made her very angry once, but that might mean she cared about him, because surely one didn't get angry with unimportant people. Or had she lost the thread of logic somewhere in following that train of thought?

' It isn't goodbye for ever,' she said, striving for lightness. ' Your home office is London, isn't it? I'll see you when you get back.'

' That might not be for weeks and weeks, the way Clark is arguing every line of every contract,' Toby said moodily. ' Valerie, stay another day or two. Please. Just for me.'

It was far too much trouble to explain that she hadn't enough money for accommodation in a European-style hotel, and that she couldn't speak the language well enough to stay in a Japanese-style hotel. Instead, looking down, she shook her head without speaking.

'Ah well,' Toby said after a moment, 'if this is to be our last evening together, let's make it one to remember.'

From then on he set himself to entertain her. He told her about the pearl culture in Toba Bay—the harvesting of 'the tears of the Queen of the Night', as the pearls were called according to an old legend. She enjoyed hearing it all, but she didn't allow herself to forget the passing of time; she must get to the airport for the ten-ten flight.

At last, catching her eye wandering once more to her wristwatch, Toby said: 'What time are you thinking of leaving?'

'I don't know. I suppose about nine o'clock. But I must get moving before then because I've got to hire a taxi and—'

'Oh, look, let me be of some use,' Toby broke in. 'I can drive you to the airport. One good thing about the way Clark tries to fit in with the local custom is that I've got a temporary licence and one of the firm's cars. It's outside now. So please do let me drive you to Haneda.'

He looked so desperately anxious about it that she agreed. They finished their coffee in leisurely fashion, before she went up to change into a lightweight flannel dress, more suitable for travelling. Then she sat down at the desk in Clark's room, took a piece of hotel notepaper, and prepared to write.

What should she say: ' Dear Clark '?—but she was angry with him still. ' Dear Mr Cummings '?—but that sounded childishly formal. In the end she simply wrote: ' Thank you for the use of the room during today. Tonight I am flying home so shall not be availing myself of it again. I enclose some money to cover the cost. Sincerely, V. Stansgate.'

After folding the note she slipped into the envelope all the *yen* notes she had left; she wouldn't be needing them any more. She kept the loose coins to buy magazines and perhaps coffee at the airport. She was rather pleased at the idea of leaving money with her note to Clark; it ought to please his businessman's instinct.

She gave the envelope to the receptionist for delivery to Clark at some future time. Outside the modern glass porch of the Azia Hotel, Toby was waiting. The page boy put her luggage in the back of the car. She got in the front seat with Toby, and off they went.

It took some time to clear the suburbs of Tokyo. Valerie sat back, watching the artificial cherry blossom on the shop fronts fall behind, glancing down side roads to see the lovely multi-coloured paper lanterns like floating baubles in front of the dark buildings.

By and by they came to open country. Paddy-fields spread on either side, towards distant hills. The countryside lay serene under a full moon, itself like some silvery lantern lit by the Queen of the Night. The road on which they were travelling was bad—the car jolted and juddered as they struck one pot-hole after another. Traffic was scanty.

After a while it began to worry Valerie. ' Are you sure we're on the right road?' she ventured. ' It seemed to me, coming to Tokyo from the airport, that the surface was better.'

' Oh, it varies.'

' But I'm sure the Tokyo monorail ran alongside. Toby, are you sure you haven't got on the wrong road?'

' It's all right,' he said reassuringly. ' I took a quieter route—I thought you'd like to look at the view.'

' Oh, I see.' She sat back; for some ten minutes longer they sped along the corrugated surface. Surreptitiously she glanced at her watch: nine-forty-five. ' Toby, I'm going to miss my plane.'

' Not to worry,' he replied. ' There'll be another one.'

' I'm not so sure about that. I didn't ask what flights there were after the one I wanted. Oh, Toby, what a nuisance! Now I shall have to hang about the airport . . .'

' I'll keep you company,' he said.

Now it was five minutes to ten, and there was no sign of the airport approach; no runway along the side of the road, no landing lights, no control tower dominating the countryside.

' Toby, where are we?'

' Oh, on our way, on our way.'

' On our way *where*?' She peered about at the

landscape. ' Toby, this isn't the way to the airport! '

He looked to one side and then the other. ' No, I'm afraid I've managed to get lost. So sorry, darling.' But he seemed completely unperturbed.

' Then stop! Stop, Toby. We can drive back the way we've come. It shouldn't be too difficult.'

' No, I suppose not, but it would be much more fun just to keep going—don't you agree?'

' Fun?' she echoed, incredulous.

' It's so romantic. There's a wonderful moon above, the most beautiful girl in the world by my side, and ahead nothing but the mountains of Japan, full of pretty little inns with waterfalls and tranquil gardens and—'

' Toby,' Valerie said in a stifled voice, ' are you out of your mind?'

' Not in the least. My brain is ticking over quite nicely. After all, what difference does it make to you whether you catch a plane tonight or tomorrow morning? We'll find some quiet little hotel, my love, on the road to Nikko, which is a famous beauty spot. I told you at dinner, didn't I, that I thought we should make your last evening one to remember.'

Horrified, Valerie stared at him. He was quite serious. He was driving with quiet concentration, his eyes on the road ahead. As he felt her gaze upon him, he turned his head, gave her a smile of reassurance, and put out a hand to pat her knee.

CHAPTER VII

It was some moments before Valerie found her voice. When at last she could speak she said: ' Turn this car round and take me to Haneda Airport.'

He shook his head. ' No, that's not the way I planned it.'

' Planned it? Do you mean to say you've actually worked out this silly idea in advance?'

' Not the details,' he confessed. ' I was a bit taken aback when you said you were flying out tonight. I expected you to stay in the hotel.'

' That would have been more convenient, of course,' she said in a tone of ice.

' True, true, but this little moonlight jaunt is very romantic, don't you agree? And it just so happened one of my Japanese business colleagues was enthusing about a heavenly little village on the road to Nikko, so I thought that would be a charming setting.'

' It didn't occur to you that I might not agree?'

' I don't see why you shouldn't.'

' Don't see why I—?' For a moment she was speechless. ' How *dare* you! What in heaven's name gave you the idea I'd fall in with this plan?'

' Oh, stop playing the injured innocent,' Toby said in a bored tone. ' After the way you've played around with Kan and Clark, you can't claim to be surprised when I want my share of the fun.'

'But . . . but . . . Kan? Kan and I . . . we were like brother and sister—not even that, for he only used his friendship with me as a part of his campaign to win Michiko. As for Clark—'

'Yes, tell me about Clark,' he broke in. 'Explain how it happens you're sharing a room with him—'

'But that's absurd! Sharing? He allowed me to use it today, that's all—'

'Oh, that's all? You must think me a fool, Val. I *saw* you. I got into Tokyo about three o'clock this afternoon and tried the handle of Clark's room to see if I could have a word with him. *And there you were!*'

Valerie felt her cheeks go hot. She remembered: the door had opened, but she had been too drowsy to rouse herself properly.

'But you don't understand,' she cried. '*He* moved out—'

'Really? His belongings were still there, I saw them. And when I opened the door you called "Clark, is that you?" If he'd moved out, why were you expecting him?'

She realized then that it would be impossible to convince Toby Bates of the innocence of the arrangement. People in general believe what they want to believe, and Toby wanted to think the worst.

Very well, let him. She didn't care one way or the other what he thought; he was beneath contempt.

'Even if what you imagine were true,' she said, 'and I absolutely deny it!—that doesn't mean I'll fall in with the present arrangement.'

146

Toby chuckled. 'You've no choice, angel. We're on our way to the Ogawa Hotel, and there's nothing you can do about it!'

'I can send for the police the minute we get there—'

'How? By speaking Japanese? What's Japanese for "policeman"? You've no idea, have you, Val? And as I think the village has about five hundred inhabitants, I shouldn't think you'd find any English-speaking university students there.' For a moment he was silent, then said: 'Come on, stop trying to be so upright and stiffnecked. We like each other, and—'

'You're quite wrong,' she said. 'I utterly despise you, and I'd rather die than let you touch me.'

'Oh, now we're having melodramatics. Val, do grow up. A girl as pretty as you must expect to attract men. If you didn't like me, why didn't you give me the cold shoulder?'

'I did like you.' She blinked back tears, determined not to cry. 'I thought you were good fun. But after this despicable, underhanded trick—'

'You'll get over it,' he replied, quite blithe. 'All's fair in love and war.'

She remembered that Clark had quoted this tag to excuse Kan's behaviour too. Kan and Toby—one was as bad as the other . . .

'Please stop the car,' she said. 'No matter what you may think, I don't want to go with you. I want to go back to Tokyo. I demand that you stop the car.'

He didn't even bother to reply to that.

Furiously, she turned the handle of the door on her side, but even as it swung open Toby had reached an arm across and slammed it. 'Don't be silly,' he said. 'I'm doing fifty, and it would do that pretty face no good at all to hit the gravel road at fifty miles an hour!'

It was only too true. The sight of the road surface rushing by had taken her breath away; even if Toby hadn't closed the door, she couldn't have jumped.

So she sat quiescent, her mind busy. No matter what Toby might say, there could be English-speaking staff at the inn. She would appeal for help. Even if they spoke no English, there must be some way . . .

Toby mistook her quietness for surrender. He gave her a smile of approval. She was tempted to turn her face away in contempt, but perhaps it was better to have him under the impression that she was 'seeing sense'.

At last some faint lights began to appear ahead. 'The Ogawa Hotel?' she queried.

'I imagine so,' he said.

And suddenly she saw an advantage. His Japanese was hardly better than her own, and she was sure that even if he could speak a little, he could not *read* it. He would have to stop and ask if this was the village of Ogawa.

They came to a crossroads and then, a little beyond it, a scatter of small timber houses, the roof of a shrine pagoda, a pond with three sleeping ducks, and a petrol station in which one light was showing. Toby slowed and took the car into the service court. 'We need petrol anyway,' he commented, and switched off.

A stocky young man in white overalls came running from the lighted office. Toby held up a hand showing four fingers, indicating four gallons. He handed out the car keys to unlock the petrol cap; after a moment, as the pump worked, he called: '*Wa doko Ogawa?*'

The sound of the pump drowned the question, which was perhaps not correctly phrased; whatever the reason, the attendant made no reply. With a mutter of irritation, Toby got out to question the man.

At that precise moment, a motor bus came cruising up the road towards the village, coming from the direction which Valerie was facing—in other words, going towards Tokyo. It was moving fast, but slid to a halt on the opposite side from the petrol station. Valerie could see two passengers queueing to alight.

Like a flash she slid across the front seat of Toby's car, under the steering wheel, and out on to the tarmac. Taking off her shoes, she ran soundlessly. The bus was revving up; she ran in front of it, waving her arms. She saw the look of astonishment in the driver's face as he saw her blonde hair and European features. The bus stopped; she threw herself aboard; the automatic door closed with a hiss. The conductor called: '*Orrye!*' and they were off.

She was safe.

Her arrival had caused quite a flutter among the other passengers. There were about twenty of them, but she was in too much of a state to pay attention to them as yet. Reaction had set in: she was trembling, her body was wet with perspiration. Her grey flannel dress was sticking to her back, she had lost a button off her poplin coat in manœuvring out of the car. But worse than all that—her head was spinning. Everything—the interior of the bus, the faces peering at her, everything—was receding into a whirling haze.

She discovered that a plastic cup was being pressed to her lips. Thinking it was *saké*, she tried to refuse. But it turned out to be tepid tea from someone's vacuum flask, so she drank it gratefully: her mouth was parched.

She looked up. The bus conductor stood back, handing the cup to its owner. '*Orrye?*' he inquired.

She nodded feebly.

He began to question her, but she spread her hands and made a little negative shake of the head. She tried to picture the words in the Japanese phrasebook she had bought after Clark had said it was important to know the polite phrases. All she could remember was '*Eigo*' which meant 'English'. She pointed to herself and said: '*Eigo.*'

Little sighs of awe and amazement greeted this. Valerie couldn't wonder at it: if the situation were reversed, and a little Japanese girl appeared out of nowhere about ten-thirty on a country road to clamber aboard a bus in a state of distress, it would cause a sensation.

The conductor smiled and bowed. He then put his hands on his ticket machine and looked inquiring. He wanted to know where she was heading.

Valerie opened her handbag, took out her purse, and tipped the coins on to the palm of her hand. 'Tokyo,' she said, offering them.

The conductor looked from her to the money, from the money to her face, then shook his head.

So it wasn't enough? Living with the Tanakas as she had done, she had never really had to grapple with the exchange situation. Alarmed now, she showed him her empty purse, then her air ticket. 'Haneda?' she said. 'Tokyo?'

He shook his head and began a long explanation, not one syllable of which meant anything to her. She sat helplessly under the torrent of words.

Now all the passengers joined in. Watching them as they conferred, Valerie sensed that they were not Tokyoans. There were more kimonos among the women, and the men, though in European clothes, wore windcheaters and jeans, not business suits. What was it Toby had said? 'I shouldn't think you'd find any English-speaking university students there.'

It came home to her at that moment how foolishly impractical she had been in her preparation for this visit. She hadn't made the slightest attempt to master the language. Somehow she had pictured herself moving always through avenues of flowers and temples, conversing with elegant Japanese who spoke perfect English. Clark had been right: her view of the country had been absurdly unrealistic. Beyond the vermilion gateway lay not only the Path of the Gods, but a multitude of ordinary people like the passengers in this bus, as unable to speak English as she was unable to speak Japanese.

There was a mutter of determination among the passengers. The owner of the vacuum flask, a young woman with a sleeping baby in the sash at her back, was pushing forward a boy of about twelve, in the black buttoned-up uniform of the schoolboy. He was clearly her elder son, and the outstanding feature about him at this moment was his unwillingness to obey.

But all his elders were issuing instructions. He hung his head, then bowed to Valerie. 'Ingrish,' he said.

She was so relieved and grateful she could have hugged him. But that would never do. She smiled at him and bowed.

'You speak English?'

He swallowed convulsively. 'Yes.' Then after promptings from his mother: 'You go . . . where?'

'Tokyo,' she said.

'No go Tokyo.' He was obviously searching for a word that he either didn't know or couldn't remember. He made a gesture with his forefinger that took in their surroundings. 'No go Tokyo.'

Valerie's heart sank. 'This bus doesn't go to Tokyo?'

'This bus!' he repeated in triumph. 'Bus no go

Tokyo.' He pointed out of the back window, his arm extended to indicate direction. 'Tokyo,' he said.

'Oh no! You mean I'm going in the wrong direction?'

The speed and emphasis of her words, and probably the words themselves, defeated him. He stood looking into her face, anxious and embarrassed, almost as perplexed as she was herself.

She realized she mustn't get in a state. The boy spoke hardly any English—most likely he was still in his first year of study in English—and to fluster him meant he would forget what he knew.

She collected her wits. She must ask her questions in the simplest form possible.

'Bus Tokyo?' she said on a strong note of interrogation.

The boy turned to the conductor and conveyed the question in a long sentence of Japanese. There was a conference among the passengers. Her interpreter returned to her task.

'Bus—' he indicated their surroundings.

'This bus,' Valerie prompted.

'This bus go to . . . houses.' He paused. 'Many some houses.'

'A village?'

This was a new word to him. 'Virrage? Some houses, one, two, three, four, houses.'

'A village,' she nodded.

'Bus Tokyo virrage.'

'You mean I can catch a bus to Tokyo from a village we're coming to?' She knew this was too

complex, and said again: ' I—' touching her chest
—' catch bus village?'—pointing ahead.

Grinning widely, he nodded. Congratulations
broke out on all sides. His mother beamed with
pride.

Valerie was smiling too. He was a good boy, and
she would have liked to reward him by giving him
some money—but perhaps that would be considered
bad form here, for there was a great sensitivity
about giving and receiving tips. Thinking of money
brought an important point to mind. She held out
the coins on her palm.

' Tokyo?' she asked.

This was a question that needed no translation.
The conductor counted the amount, hesitated, then
said, ' *Saa, orrye.*' Which seemed to mean that
it would probably be enough.

The bus trundled on over the bumpy road.
Valerie sat back and allowed herself a moment's
triumphant speculation over Toby's feelings when
he turned around and found her gone. How soon
had he missed her? Had he seen her climb aboard
the bus? Whether or no, he would have been unable
to follow for at least some minutes, for the petrol
cap would have to be locked on and the ignition
key returned and the petrol paid for—three or four
minutes at least. By that time the bus would have
covered about a mile and probably taken one of the
many little side-roads. She glanced back through
the rear window. No sign of headlights. In any
case he could hardly give chase; what good would

it do him? Only physical force would have made her accompany him now, and he could hardly get rough in front of a busload of people.

But on the debit side . . . She had lost all her luggage. It was in the back of Toby's car. All her clothes, and her notebooks and sketchbooks of Ikebana, and her souvenirs: all of them were in her two suitcases.

What would Toby do with them? If he had any decency he would take them to Haneda Airport so that when she eventually caught a flight home her luggage would catch up with her.

But she seriously doubted now whether Toby had any sense of fitness. He was too bound up in his own view of things, too immersed in his own wishes and desires. To have imagined that she would fall in with his warped ideas . . . ! No, not even that —she was to have had no choice. He took it for granted that she would agree, or submit, or even co-operate.

The strange thing was that she wasn't angry— not angry as she had been with Clark for grabbing and kissing her. All she felt for Toby was a dreary disgust. He wasn't worth any more than that— a silly, empty man functioning behind a façade of good manners and good looks.

One or two lights began to shimmer on the road ahead. The bus's speed decreased. The conductor nodded to her, saying: ' Kemusiki,' and then gesturing towards the door.

She got up, discovered to her astonishment that

she had no shoes on; they were on the seat beside her. She put them on, moved to the exit. No one else was getting off here. Her friendly little boy rose to bow farewell.

' *Arigato*,' she said, returning his bow.

His face split in an enormous, sleepy grin. He bowed again. He and the conductor handed her down at the bus stop. The bus moved off.

' *Sayonara!* ' called the boy. ' *Sayonara*, Engrish!'

The last she saw, he was hanging out of the window waving.

She looked about her, and all at once she wanted to run after the bus, call it back. The village seemed almost totally asleep. Lights still shone from behind the paper windows of one or two cottages, but the general effect was of a place tucked up for the night.

The road ran through the village and then turned to the right, where she could see fields and trees glimmering under the moon. She could count about twelve houses, and two shops. There were gardens with fruit trees, their pale blossom silvery in the night. As she watched, a man on a little Honda scooter came putt-putting down the road, past her, and on into the countryside. A dog barked. Nothing else stirred.

The bus stop consisted of a concrete pole bearing a sign with Japanese characters. A little way back from the road stood a noticeboard with what was perhaps a timetable; she approached it, and turned away in despair—Japanese script.

There was nothing to do but wait for the bus.

The mild, cloudy day had turned to a clammy night. A faint breeze moved the trees, a slight mist was rising from the earth. She turned up the collar of her coat against the dampness, leaned against the signpost.

The minutes dragged by. She held her wrist up towards the moonlight and tried to read the time: it looked like ten to eleven, as far as she could make out.

No sound of traffic, no footsteps, nothing. One of the lights went out in the house farther up the road. Panic began to mount inside her—perhaps she should run to the other house where there was a light, before it too went out, and ask—What?

She couldn't say anything in Japanese except 'Please' and 'Thank you', 'Hello' and 'Goodbye'. How was she to say 'When is the next bus to Tokyo?'

But still—when that light went out she would be alone—alone here in this alien countryside, unable to communicate, practically penniless, tired, frightened and lost. Wouldn't it be better to knock on a door like a beggar than to shiver out here like a dog?

She was summoning up her courage to move when, from the house with the light, two people emerged. Their footsteps sounded loud in the quiet village. They were walking towards the bus stop.

Coming to catch the last bus to Tokyo?

Her heart gave a great leap of hope and reassurance. She stood up straighter, prepared to bow and try to make conversation when they joined her. Now they were more distinct under the hazy moonlight —an elderly couple, the woman in kimono and the thick wooden-soled sandals called *geta*, the man in a gaberdine raincoat and heavy shoes. Both had grey hair; they walked with rather short, sedate steps.

She could see they had spotted her; they were staring at her with the undisguised wonder her appearance seemed to arouse everywhere. They came towards her, eyes glued on her face, commenting to each other in low, astonished voices. They came abreast.

And then, to her utter horror, they walked past her and on towards the open fields.

Valerie was so shattered that she couldn't even speak. She watched, numb with shock, as they trudged away from her, casting occasional incredulous glances over their shoulders. She felt a terrible sob rising in her throat, childish and betraying. She struggled against it, for if once she began to cry she knew she would never stop. She put her fist up to her mouth and bit the knuckles, determined to prevent a hysterical outburst.

The ground mist was growing thicker now. The moon was veiled so that everything glimmered in a vague grey light. She could just discern that the old couple had stopped some yards away, and a discussion was going on. The old lady's voice, thin and insistent, carried more easily than the man's.

A moment later they came clearly into view, the

old gentleman walking a pace or two ahead of his wife. When he was within a few feet of Valerie, he bowed. She returned his bow, swallowing hard so that she would be able to speak.

She had no idea what he said, but when he finished on a note of inquiry she pointed to herself and said: '*Eigo.*'

The old man bowed, repeated his question.

She shook her head. '*Eigo.* Bus Tokyo.' She pointed.

'Tokyo?' he repeated. Next came a stream of information which meant nothing to her. All she could do was point to the bus stop, to herself, and to the direction in which she wanted to travel.

He shook his head vigorously saying something that sounded like: '*Rakusi han.*' He pointed to her wristwatch, then at the timetable. At his beckoning gesture she went with him to the noticeboard. He pointed to the last line on the placard, waved a hand towards the road, then moved his pointing finger to the top of the column. '*Rakusi han,*' he repeated, holding up six fingers, then adding a little chopping motion.

She understood. Only too well, she understood. Half past six tomorrow morning. The last bus for tonight had already gone.

She nodded and said, '*Arigato.*'

He smiled, bowed, and walked away, his duty done.

What was she to do? There were seven and a half hours to wait. Where was she to go?

The elderly couple were moving away. Should she call them back, ask if there was a hotel? What was Japanese for hotel? Clark had said the word . . . *'Rookya'? 'Koorya'? 'Yoorka'?* She had no idea. Besides, had she enough to pay for a hotel?

Now the couple had stopped again, were staring at her. The old lady was talking vehemently; the old man was looking at the ground, apparently unwilling. All at once the old lady darted round him and came hurrying back, her *geta* thudding on the gravel road. She stopped by the bus stop.

They exchanged the inevitable bows. The old lady's hand, moth-like in the dark, fluttered towards the road. She shook her head as she said: *'Basu wa arimasen.'* It came to Valerie that this perhaps meant 'There is no bus.' She nodded to say she understood. Her new friend now asked a question, waited for a reply, and getting none went on to repeat it with explanatory mime. She put her hands together palm inwards, laid them against her cheek with her head tilted, and closed her eyes.

She was asking if Valerie had anywhere to sleep.

Despite herself, two tears trickled on to her cheeks. She looked down, ashamed, wiping them away with her knuckles as she shook her head.

The old lady made a sound that quite clearly meant, 'Poor child.' A little bony hand came under Valerie's chin, tilting her face upwards. Then, smiling, she took her by the arm and pulled gently.

Valerie was only too happy to go with her. The

old gentleman fell into step on the other side and all three walked slowly in the direction the two old people had originally been going. Valerie could see nothing ahead except fields, but in a moment they took a path off to the left, which eventually curved round by the side of a brook, through a little orchard, and up to the door of a cottage. The man opened the door, switched on a light, and ushered her in.

The main living-room lay immediately ahead of her. She slipped off her shoes and walked in. Her hostess took her coat, offered cushions, trotted away to a room beyond from which the sound of a kettle singing could soon be heard. Her host sat down opposite her.

'Aiko,' he said, tapping his chest.

'Valerie,' she replied, doing likewise.

He nodded and smiled, revealing several gold teeth. He flicked a hand towards the clock on the wall, then rubbed his eyes and yawned, implying that it was late and he was sleepy. She nodded agreement. He laughed, murmured a few words, then made eating motions with a glance towards the kitchen. He called: 'Kazuko!'

His wife appeared. He made eating motions again and issued an order, to which she replied in obvious indignation that the food was coming. A few minutes later she brought in a tray with tea and a plate covered with a paper napkin. She poured the tea, laid it on the matting in front of Valerie, and then with an air of triumph whipped away the paper napkin to offer the plate to her guest.

On it lay a sponge jam sandwich, like any of a hundred Valerie's mother had made for Sunday tea at home in Manchester. At sight of it, so comically incongruous in this exotic setting, Valerie began to laugh—and once having begun, she couldn't stop. She laughed until the tears ran down her cheeks, and until the laughter turned to sobs, and Mrs Aiko put her arms round her and patted her soothingly, and at last, spent and ashamed, she was calm again.

Mrs Aiko made her eat and drink. She felt better after that—less tense but extremely weary. Her hostess beckoned her to follow, took her to a bath-house at the side of the cottage, gave her a thin rough towel and a white sleeping kimono. When she had washed and got ready for bed she came back into the house; sleeping mats had been laid out for her in a corner of a room that seemed to be a farm store-room. Mrs Aiko tucked her in and flitted silently away.

Valerie told herself she should have said thank-you and asked to be taken to the bus stop in time for the six-thirty bus. But leaden weights seemed to be tied to her limbs and her tongue and her eyelids; her thought processes had become as slow as hibernating animals. Too exhausted to cope with any more, she slid down into an abyss of sleep.

CHAPTER VIII

When she awoke Mrs Aiko was shaking her gently by the shoulder. She sat up, wondering where she was; then as recollection returned she glanced at her watch—but she had forgotten to wind it last night and it showed twenty past three.

She could tell by the light that it was still early. She said: 'Is it half-past six?' but Mrs Aiko shook her head in incomprehension. She had Valerie's clothes over her arm; she pointed to them, then towards the bath-house, and flicked with her hands to let her know she should hurry to wash and dress.

Valerie hastened to obey. Her mind was working clearly again this morning. Once she got to Tokyo she would find the airline offices and be taken by airline transport to Haneda for the plane. If there was a charge for the transport, she would promise to pay by sterling at the other end, once she was safely home. If they were doubtful about it, she had her airline ticket and her passport as bona fides. She would be provided with meals on the plane. When she landed she would ring her parents and ask them to come and collect her. They would be surprised —particularly if she still hadn't got back her luggage —but there was no need to distress them by going into all the reasons for her sudden return.

She came back into the house, the sleeping kimono folded over her arm, braced to face the undoubted

163

difficulties of this new day. As she came into the living-room she discovered that the Aikos were entertaining guests. A young, thin girl in European dress and an older man in a smart uniform with white gloves were there.

The girl moved forward. 'Miss Stansgate? I am Miss Hidato and this is Sergeant Geigin, of the police.'

'Police?' said Valerie. 'But why—?'

'Your friends have been very anxious all night. This morning Sergeant Geigin received telephone call, to say probably Miss Stansgate is here in Kemusiki, will to please find. Sergeant Geigin ask at houses, find Mr Aiko invite you, then comes as instructed to school to find teacher speaking English. I do not speak good,' she added, blushing, 'but try very hard.'

'You speak it excellently,' Valerie cried. 'But who rang the sergeant? How could anyone know where I was?'

Miss Hidato translated this to the sergeant who, smiling with satisfaction, gave her an explanation.

'Sergeant says your friend found bus conductor who showed you bus stop in Kemusiki. Very many telephonings before Mr Cummings find bus conductor.'

'Mr Cummings!' breathed Valerie.

'Sergeant has telephone message to ask you, please remain here with Aikos, eat breakfast. Mr Cummings is here soon to drive you to Tokyo. Sergeant asked me to write down telephone message for you from Mr Cummings.' She held out a piece of paper.

In the strange angular writing of Miss Hidato, Valerie read: ' Your whereabouts established 5.30 a.m. Am on my way, probably arriving 7 a.m. Please don't take off into the unknown again. Clark.'

It was terse, peremptory, with a note of reproof—the kind of note a headmaster would write to an errant sixth-former. She was stung by it, yet the thought of having Clark there to ease all her difficulties was compensation enough. She turned to Miss Hidato.

' What time is it now, please?'

' Six-forty-five. Mr Cummings should be here soon, although this is not a main road.'

The situation had already been explained to the Aikos, it seemed, for Mrs Aiko threw herself into a frenzy of preparation. Pans and dishes crashed about in the kitchen, savoury smells of rice and fish and soy sauce began to drift about. Mr Aiko sat down, took out his pipe, and had a peaceful pre-breakfast smoke. The sergeant, clearly delighted with the excitement brought to his area, bowed and went out to watch for the European visitor. Miss Hidato sat down beside Valerie to explain that she taught in the junior school for the district, situated in the next village.

About ten minutes later there were footsteps on the path. Valerie felt herself colouring, her pulse heightening.

The sergeant came in, followed by Clark. As always, he dwarfed everyone else in the room. He gave Valerie a brief glance, then at once, as courtesy demanded, greeted the owner of the house and his wife, and then Miss Hidato, to whom he had already spoken on the phone.

'I apologize for getting you out of bed so early, Miss Hidato,' he said.

'It was a great honour to be asked to help.'

'I am very grateful, I assure you. Can I show my appreciation in any way? Could I be of service to you or your school?'

'You are very kind, Mr Cummings,' she said, going pink with pleasure. 'I will ask my principal . . .'

'Here is my business card. I'll write to you in a day or two to see what has been decided.'

At last he turned his attention on Valerie. 'Well,' he said, 'so there you are. For a girl who speaks no Japanese you have a way of getting around.'

It was difficult to tell from his tone whether he was angry or exasperated or simply tired. He *looked* tired, his face rather pale under the tan; shadows under his eyes.

'I'm sorry to keep being a nuisance,' Valerie said. 'It's kind of you to have taken all this trouble.'

'Not kind at all,' he said brusquely. 'If an employee of my company gets involved in an alarming situation like this, it's up to me to sort it out.'

'Oh, I see.'

Mrs Aiko began bringing in food. Almost like a dutiful daughter, Miss Hidato sprang to her assistance. In a few minutes the whole party was sitting round the low table, attacking the array of little dishes and bowls which held the contents of a Japanese breakfast.

Rather to Valerie's surprise, Clark ate heartily and held a spirited conversation with Mr Aiko and the sergeant. Valerie found she was expected to concentrate her attention on the two women, which proved difficult because Miss Hidato wanted to practise her English, of which Mrs Aiko knew nothing.

At last the meal ended. Polite goodbyes were said. Like a procession they all wended their way down the path to the road. Everything sparkled in the morning sunlight; last night's mist had left a dew on the foliage so that every leaf, every twig, sparkled like diamanté. A bird sang a repeated, trilling song. In the fields workers in conical straw hats were already bending over the rice lines. In the distance a mountain rose, less perfect than Fujiyama but more rugged, more commanding.

Clark helped her in, gave a last bow all round and a handshake to the sergeant as well, then got into the car and drove off. Neither of them spoke for some minutes.

'Could I ask how you found out where I was?' she ventured at last.

'We worked out that you must have got on the bus. It was the only solution. So we—'

'We? Who's "we"? You and Toby?'

He turned a flinty glance on her, his brows a straight, dark, frowning line. 'I wouldn't discuss cents in a dollar with Toby Bates after this. No, the Tokyo police and I.'

'How did the police come into it?'

'I called them in, for heaven's sake! What did you expect? That I could let you vanish into the night in the middle of the Japanese countryside?'

At the rasp of anger in his voice she hung her head. 'I'm sorry. I know you think I'm a fool. But I don't really understand how you knew . . . ?'

'I'll go back to the beginning,' he said. 'I came back to the hotel last night to apologize.' He bit his lip. 'I'm sorry about that pass I tried to make.'

'That's all right. I was silly to get upset.' She wanted to say that, compared to what had happened since, Clark's behaviour seemed at least open and straightforward. But she didn't dare.

'I got your note,' Clark said.

Memory came flooding back: the cold words, the insult implied by the inclusion of money. Oh, how could she have done that? Overcome with shame and remorse, she said nothing.

'The clerk told me you'd driven away with Toby, so I hung about to ask him if you'd caught your plane okay. When he came in . . . well, one look at him and you could see something had gone wrong.' Clark stared grimly through the windscreen, and sounded his horn angrily at a dog who trotted across the road. 'He said at first he'd seen you off, but . . . I don't know, he was so jittery

I knew he had something on his conscience. But to tell the truth I thought he'd maybe had an accident with the car—Tokyo traffic is a bit chaotic. I went out to have a look at it—it's a company car, you know. And then . . .' he hesitated . . . 'I saw your luggage in the back.'

There was no doubt he had had a shock at that moment. The pallor of his face now, as he recalled it, was evidence of that.

'Well, then I got it out of him—at least, *his* version. What actually happened, Valerie?'

'What does he say happened?'

'That he lost his way en route to the airport. You had a quarrel and you got out and ran off.'

'Well, let's say that's near enough.'

'Confound it, Valerie, it isn't enough. I'm responsible for that man—he's an employee of the firm in which I hold a senior post. I want the truth.'

Valerie experienced a strange sense of disappointment; but after all it was only logical that Clark should put the business reputation of his firm first. Yet she didn't want to discuss last night's episode. She let the silence prolong itself.

'Look here, it's quite clear he's lying. If he was driving you to the airport, what was he doing twenty miles the other side of Tokyo?'

'Well,' she said unwillingly, 'let's put it this way. I thought we were driving to the airport, but when I found out where we were actually heading, I decided I didn't care for it. So I took the first chance I got, and cleared out.'

'Huh,' he grunted. 'You never wanted to go with him?'

'Only to the airport.'

He nodded. 'According to him it was all a great mistake and you just ran off out of mischief. But I remembered that time in Tokyo when you got lost —I *knew* you wouldn't do a thing like that again except under extreme provocation. Well, he told me where you'd disappeared. He guessed you'd got on the bus, although he didn't actually see you. But do you know what that weak-kneed, selfish fool did then? He just drove back to the Azia Hotel. He said he didn't see what point there was in making a fuss. It didn't occur to him that you were adrift without money in a totally alien environment. Or maybe it did, but he felt he'd be in trouble if he reported it.'

Valerie sighed. 'He's not really my favourite man at the moment,' she said. 'But in actual fact I didn't come to any harm.'

'No?' Did you enjoy yourself, then? No fears or anxieties?' Clark's voice was sharp. 'I spoke to the conductor of the bus you boarded. He said you were very distressed.'

'Well, I . . . Yes, I suppose I was, but it all ended all right.'

'I can't take your view. Toby Bates is intending to take up a very responsible job in my firm, a job where character counts for as much as brains. Oh, he's clever, all right—he can pick flaws out of a contract quicker than a hen pecking corn. But what

170

about a sense of responsibility, a regard for the wellbeing of someone or something other than himself? No, he's a washout. Soon as you're safe in Tokyo I'm going into my office and dictate a recommendation that we dispense with his services as soon as possible. I hope he comes complaining to me about it,' he added grimly. ' I'll be happy to tell him he's lucky he's not on a charge of abduction.'

He sounded so deeply angry that Valerie wouldn't have dared plead for Toby, even if she had thought he deserved it.

' When did you contact the bus conductor?' she asked. ' He was nice.'

' We ran him to earth about twelve-thirty last night. I rang the police about an hour earlier, saying that a lady tourist had got on a wrong bus by mistake and could they find out *which* bus. I was able to give them the time and the place you boarded, so they checked at once and gave us the conductor. He lived in a little village on the coast north of Tokyo. We had to roust him out of bed. Poor chap, he was scared stiff—thought he was being accused of some crime.'

' Oh, poor man! He took so much trouble—'

' I know, I know—we sorted it all out. I spoke to him myself—'

' On the phone?'

' No, in person. I had hoped you'd stayed on the bus to the terminus, but of course I didn't find you there—I was told you'd got off at Kemusiki. The police were very helpful. They got their area sergeant to go from house to house as soon as daylight began—people around here are early risers, you see. By five-thirty he'd rung back to say the Aikos had taken you in for the night. I asked him to find someone who could speak English, so he produced Miss Hidato to act as interpreter. The rest you know.'

'I've caused a lot of trouble,' she said repentantly. 'Everything I've done since I got here has gone wrong. It's a good thing I'm going home today.'

He gave her a sharp, brief glance. 'You intend to leave?'

'Well, there's nothing to stay for, is there?'

'No, I suppose not.'

They drove in silence from then on until they reached the outskirts of Tokyo. Here Clark said, 'Look, Valerie, I contacted Michiko. I thought it would be better if you went there. I mean, I can't exactly turn Toby out of his hotel, so if I take you there you might run into him—and I take it you'd rather not?'

Valerie made no reply, only shivered.

'Right. I'm afraid the Misumis' house was the only other place I could think of. Kan may turn up there, of course, but I could have a word with Michiko . . . ?'

'No, no,' she said. 'I've caused enough trouble. No, if Michiko will take me in for a few hours, until I can arrange my flight . . .'

'Okay. So that's where we're headed.'

It was the morning rush hour in Tokyo. Traffic was indescribably chaotic, so that Clark could drive only at a snail's pace. Watching his patient manœuvring, Valerie said, ' Don't you lose your temper, having to deal with this sort of thing?'

' No,' he said. ' It's another of the facets of the Japanese character—they can't control their traffic. But as I told you, when you're in a strange country you have to accept their ways, even though you may not approve.' They inched along.

Valerie thought Michiko would have left for the boutique, but no—she came flying out of the house as they drew up.

' Valerie, you are all right? We have been so worried—'

' Oh yes,' Clark put in, ushering her in. ' I brought your cases here last night on my way to see the busman. I expected to bring you home about an hour later, but of course it didn't work out like that.'

' Oh, Michiko, how awful! I wouldn't have alarmed you for the world.'

Mrs Misumi came to greet her, laughing and bowing and wiping tears away all at once. The little house looked cosy and welcoming; an Ikebana arrangement, exquisitely fragile, stood on the special shelf below the scroll showing a spring landscape. The mimosa's perfume filled the room. A low table was ready to receive the tea-tray. Mrs Misumi made a gesture of invitation, but Clark, in a carefully polite speech, excused himself.

'I've got to get to the office,' he reminded Valerie, his mouth grim. 'I'll never rest easy till I've written that report. So I'll push off now. So long, Valerie.'

'Shall I see you again?' she asked, feeling suddenly bereft.

'Sure. Let me know what plane you're taking and I'll come and wave goodbye.'

'Oh. Yes, all right, I will.'

Michiko had been given the day off when she explained to her employer that her fair-haired European friend was in some trouble and needed her. She sat in a leisurely fashion over the tea-things looking, Valerie thought, quietly radiant.

It could only be because of Kan, and though in a Japanese girl it would have been bad manners to ask, Valerie had no such reserve. 'Did you see Kan yesterday?' she asked bluntly.

Michiko blushed. 'Yes, he came here in the evening. We had a long talk. He told me, Valerie, that Clark-*san* had been angry with him, that he had caused you great distress.' Michiko's hands trembled as she put them up to her face. 'He explained to me what all his strange behaviour of the last few weeks had meant.'

'He told you he loved you?'

Michiko bent her head so that her brows met her finger tips, thus hiding her face. 'Yes,' she whispered.

'Well, don't be so upset about it,' Valerie urged, laughing. 'I'd have thought you'd feel like jumping over the moon!'

' Please?'

' It's an English expression, meaning "to feel great happiness ". You are happy, aren't you, Michiko?'

' Ye . . . es,' she agreed. ' But uneasy too. His parents will not approve.'

' I think they will. They'll think you're a vastly better choice than me.'

' Yes,' Michiko agreed innocently, ' but I am not the daughter-in-law they would really choose.'

' So if they say "No, not on any account!" you'll give Kan up?' asked Valerie, knowing very well what the answer would be.

Michiko shook her head. ' I could not. Not now. I hope and pray Dr and Mrs Tanaka will give their agreement, and if they do I hope they will come to approve of me in time. But if Kan asks me to marry him without his parents' consent, I think I would do it.' She gave a shy smile. ' I think you have made me *modan*, Valerie!'

' Well, that's one good thing I've achieved, anyway,' Valerie said. And, even though her role in this matchmaking hadn't been exactly to her taste, she couldn't help thinking it had worked out very well. Michiko was just the kind of wife Kan needed: ' *modan* ' enough to keep alongside him in his career but docile and gentle so that she would never argue with him. She was a mingling of the East and the West, exactly calculated to please a quick, clever, slightly unscrupulous young man like

Kan. His parents, Valerie was sure, would soon learn to love Michiko—they would have to be monsters not to appreciate her goodness and sweetness. Mrs Tanaka would come round before her husband did; he was stubborn and autocratic; but he was human and would give in after a suitable interval.

Oh, it was all very satisfactory. Valerie couldn't imagine herself loving anyone who had done something so devious as Kan, but if Michiko was happy that was all that mattered.

They discussed what to do next, as they finished their tea. Valerie wanted to go to the airline office to see about a flight; Michiko suggested they should walk there, since it was such a beautiful day. ' And then,' she said, blushing, ' I agreed to meet Kan for lunch. He thought, of course, that I would be at work today. So we were to meet at the bridge to the Imperial Palace.'

' Well, you can do that and I can take a streetcar home—'

' Oh no, come with me, Valerie. Come and meet Kan. He was so sad last night that you would not see him and let him apologize.'

' No, I—'

' Please, Valerie.'

It was impossible to refuse. So, some three hours later, they strolled on to the bridge that crosses the moat to the pine-clad ramparts of the Imperial Palace, and there was Kan, in blue shirt and blue jeans, lithe as a whip and very handsome.

' Valerie!' he cried. ' I thought you flew home

last night!'

'No, I had a change of plan.'

He said: 'That's great, because all morning I've been trying to write you a letter saying how sorry I am for all the upset I caused, and I haven't gotten on with it at all well.' He paused, and grew more serious. 'Valerie, I didn't really mean things to go the way they did. I'd no idea my father would take the bit between his teeth and order you out.'

'But when he did, you decided to turn it to your own advantage,' she replied tartly.

'Well . . . yes. It would have been silly to waste the chance.'

'I don't see that, Kan. I think your best plan would have been to go to your father and say: "Make your mind easy. It's not Valerie I'm interested in, it's Michiko." '

'But if I'd done that, he'd have been very angry and forbidden me to see Michiko.'

'And you could have disobeyed him.'

The sentence dropped between them, like a stone in a pool, sending circles of wider and wider disturbance.

'Defy him openly?' Kan said.

'Why not? You're a man, not a child. And in wanting to marry Michiko you're not doing anything wrong.'

Kan looked amazed and Michiko looked distressed.

'I'm sorry,' Valerie said. 'I oughtn't to talk like this. You understand your own social set-up better than I do, and I've no business to interfere. In any case it's all academic now, because presumably when you ask your father about marrying Michiko now, he'll agree.'

' I guess he will,' Kan said.

' And though perhaps you are right, Valerie,' Michiko put in, ' I would not like to cause a break between Kan and his father. To us that is a terrible thing. I would rather Dr Tanaka gave his consent.'

' Then that's fine.'

' But what you said,' Kan remarked slowly, ' is worth thinking of. There's a lot I still don't know, it seems—things you can't learn in a university seminar . . .'

They had lunch in an amicable threesome. Then, as she had promised, Valerie rang Clark's office to say that her plane took off at nineteen hundred hours.

' Michiko and Kan are taking me to the airport,' she said, so that he would know he didn't need to come if he didn't want to.

' Mind if I drop by for a minute as well? I've got something for you.'

' You have? What is it?'

' Oh, a little going away present. See you at Haneda.'

They went by monorail to the airport, an experience in itself. ' The world's most modern railway,' Kan said proudly. It whisked them there in record time.

Clark was already there, having driven straight

from his office. 'Hello,' he said, 'had a good day?'

'Yes, thank you, lovely.'

'You look a bit tired.'

'But then so do you.'

'Oh, well, you know the phrase "a tired businessman".'

'That's what *geisha* were invented for,' Kan suggested, laughing.

Michiko touched his arm and led him away to look at a showcase full of Japanese dolls. Clark watched them go, then took a box from the inside breast pocket of his jacket. 'I thought you might like this,' he said, 'as a souvenir.'

She opened the box. Inside lay a slender bracelet, only millimetres wide, made of gold filigree set with tiny seed pearls.

'Oh, Clark,' she said. 'How *beautiful*! But you shouldn't . . .'

'Compliments of the Lustre Jewel Company,' he said awkwardly. 'It's the Rukos' latest design.'

'Oh, I see . . .' A peace offering from the company so that she wouldn't think too harshly of them and their employees. 'Well, thank you very much.' She put it in her bag.

'It's a pleasure.'

They stood in stilted silence. Michiko and Kan had gone inside the shop. Valerie looked wildly round for them, hoping for rescue.

'What happened about Toby? Did you put in your report?'

Clark grimaced. 'No, he beat me to it. Sent in

a letter of resignation, said he didn't think spending so much time in Japan would suit him. He flew out this morning.'

'Oh . . . Well, that's just as well, really, don't you think?'

Clark shrugged.

Kan and Michiko reappeared carrying a parcel in beautifully gay paper.

'Oh, so there you are,' Clark said. 'I'll leave Valerie in your hands, then.' He turned, held out his hand. 'So long, Valerie. Take care.'

'So long, Clark. Thanks for everything.'

He gave her a little wave and walked away. Curiously, she felt as if something inside her were dying.

'We bought you a present!' Kan exclaimed in boisterous delight. 'A souvenir of Japan.'

'Clark just gave me a present,' Valerie said. 'Look.' She showed them the seed pearl bracelet; it blurred before her eyes.

'That's pretty,' Kan said. 'But open ours, open ours!'

She undid the wrapping. Inside was a beautifully dressed *geisha* doll, her kimono of pale pink silk embroidered with gold thread, her head dressed high with ivory pins.

'Oh, it's lovely,' said Valerie, staring at it, scarcely seeing it.

'Do you like it? Really?'

'Yes, Kan, it's gorgeous.'

'Kan,' said Michiko, 'would you go and check

that there's no flight delay?'

Kan stared at her. 'They'd announce it over the loudspeakers—'

'But would you please make sure?'

Kan looked at her. 'Sure,' he said, mystified, and went.

Michiko drew Valerie to a nearby seat. 'May I ask a very personal, impolite question?' she inquired.

Valerie's eyes widened. 'Of course.'

'English girls,' said Michiko, 'do not have trouble about being in love? They can love who they like?'

'Well . . . yes.'

'No one stops them?'

'No. I told you that before, Michiko.'

'No one stops *you*? You do not have to have agreement of father and mother in England?'

'No, certainly not.'

'English man the same?'

'Yes, just the same.'

'Then why,' exclaimed Michiko, 'do you not tell Clark-*san* you love him, and why does he not tell you? Why do you fly away without a word when you are dying of unhappiness and so is he?'

Valerie felt all the colour drain from her face. 'What?' she faltered. 'Michiko, how can you—? Clark doesn't love *me*!'

'No? Last night, when he came to leave your luggage and then go to find you, his face is like silk that will tear in two with strain. His eyes—so anxious! He could not speak, he was so worry. Today he brings you my house . . . he watches you, afraid you disappear again—'

'But, Michiko—'

'And tonight here,' Michiko swept on inexorably. 'You do not see his eyes? Sadness too deep for easy words.'

'But—oh, you can't mean it! He's never said anything—'

'And you, have you said anything? I do not hear you say words. He gives present, you say "Thank you". He was saying "Here is my life" and you should say also "Here is mine"—but you say "Thank you"—from the shop window I watched, and I do not understand, for English girls can speak and I waited to see you speak. Why did you not speak, Valerie?'

Kan came back. 'There's no delay,' he said, and was immediately drowned out by the loudspeakers calling for the passengers to go through the departure gate.

'Goodbye, Valerie,' he said, taking her in his arms and hugging her. 'Goodbye, and thank you. Michiko and I will let you know when we are to be married—maybe we'll come to see you on our honeymoon.'

'Yes, I . . . Goodbye, Kan. Goodbye, Michiko.' She hugged and kissed them both, then went with the little crowd of passengers through the departure gate.

'Goodbye!' called Kan. '*Sayonara!*'

She waved and walked on.

'Why did you not speak, Valerie?' Michiko's question beat in her ears as she walked down the corridor.

'Because I didn't know, Michiko!' she cried within herself. 'Until you said it, I didn't know!'

All these weeks, almost from the very first moment she saw him, her regard for him had been growing while she was quite unaware of it. Convinced they saw things from different angles, she had never thought of him as someone who could mean anything in her life. But the moment real troubles and doubts began to crowd in, to whom had she turned?

Oh, it was true she had had fights with him. And when he kissed her, she had been angry. Yet why? Only because it had meant so much to her, and at the time she had been sure she couldn't let him get away with a thing like that.

But in her heart she had always liked him more than anyone else, respected him more, felt more faith and trust than in any other man she had known. It was true, she loved him.

What good did it do to know it now? It was too late. In a moment she would be airborne, speeding back towards the West, towards the opposite side of the world. She would never see him again. It was too late.

Then suddenly she stopped. Too late? Never!

She began to battle her way back through the crowd of passengers, back towards the doors through which she had just come.

'Madame!' cried the little air hostess in charge of them. 'You're going the wrong way!'

'That's what you think!' Valerie panted.

Free of the knot of people, she ran. She pushed through the doors and into the departure lounge. Kan and Michiko were standing much where she had left them.

'What's the matter, Valerie?' Kan exclaimed, starting forward in alarm.

Michiko caught his arm to keep him from getting in Valerie's way. Paying him no heed, Valerie swept past. She ran to the doorway through which Clark had gone.

But he was not in the big entrance hall. Her heart seemed to change into a shaft of pain in her chest.

'Clark!' she cried, almost on a sob. But there was no one to answer to that name among the people in the hall.

He would have gone to his car. She caught at the jacket of a passing official.

'Where is the car park, please?' she asked, and held her breath for fear he would return a look of blank incomprehension.

'Out of the entrance and to the left, madam,' he replied in perfect English.

She ran. He might drive away before she could reach him. But the car park was not far and she could see no tall European figure among the people moving there, nor could she identify the Honda among the models in the parking lines.

She stood hesitating. Had he already gone? Oh, no, surely not—there hadn't been time, and he had been moving slowly when he walked away. She herself had only let a few minutes elapse since Michiko challenged her, and before that, not more than five minutes had gone by since Clark said good-bye. At the most, ten minutes. Could he have left the terminal inside ten minutes?

Then all at once she knew where she would find him.

If Michiko was right in saying Clark loved her—and her heart told her this was so—Clark would not have left the airport until he had seen her plane take safely to the air.

He would be on the observation platform. He would watch the jet taxi down the runway and take off, and then he would leave, knowing that the last bond between them was severed.

She followed the signs in English directing viewers to the observation roof. As she climbed the stairs, she heard the whine of the jet engine rising to take-off pitch, and pictured the plane heading down into the wind for flight. Breathless already, she tried to move faster; Clark would think she was *on that plane* —she must get to him at once, to let him know everything was all right.

But she was still climbing when she saw little groups of people coming towards her after watching the take-off. She stopped. Her eyes were riveted on that tall, commanding presence silhouetted against the lights at the top of the staircase. She stood stock still, gripping the handrail, unable to move.

' Clark!' she called.

She couldn't see his face—he was in silhouette. But she saw him freeze at the sound of her voice, saw his head come up as he tried to identify the direction of the sound.

' Clark, I'm here!'

He moved like a lion springing. Taking the stairs five at a time, he reached her. As he came, she took her hand from the rail and held it out towards him; the other held her handbag and the absurd doll that Kan had bought, and some magazines.

Next moment bag, doll and papers went scattering on the staircase as Clark swept her up. The impetus of his movement was too great to be stopped, he simply picked her up and carried her down to the hall.

' Valerie,' he said, holding her in a fierce grip as he steadied himself. ' Valerie, *Valerie*.'

She hid her face against his shoulder for a moment, breathing the familiar scent of cigarette tobacco, castile soap and worsted jacket that was the masculine aura of the man she loved. Then she looked up at him.

' Clark, I couldn't go without saying thank you for my lovely bracelet: I want to give you something in return.'

He looked into her face, the green-flecked eyes brilliant with understanding. ' This?' he asked, and kissed her.

She lost herself in that kiss, lost for ever the Valerie Stansgate of the years that had been, and found in exchange the new, complete personality that would be hers, come what might, for the rest of her life—Clark's girl, the girl who loved Clark. Nothing else seemed to matter now, only the fact that she was in the arms of the man she loved—unexpectedly, undeservedly, but oh, so happily.

At last she became aware of sound around them. Unwillingly Clark let her go. Polite Japanese faces appeared at Clark's elbow. Voices murmured. She was being offered the possessions Clark had swept away in his onslaught.

'*Arigato*,' she said. '*Arigato, arigato*.'

The contents of her bag had scattered. She was given her passport and airline ticket, and then the slim box containing the bracelet. She opened it. The fragile circle lay on its velvet bed. She took it out and handed it to Clark.

'Put it on for me,' she begged, blushing.

He took her hand and slid the bracelet over her fingers to her wrist. 'With this ring,' he quoted. He too had coloured, but his eyes were dancing. 'With this ring, I thee tether. *Please* don't go anywhere again without me, Valerie. I'm no softie, but much more of this and I'll be a nervous wreck.'

'I won't,' she promised.

'I thought you were on that plane. I thought you'd flown out of my life!'

'Not me, only my luggage.' She was struck with

consternation. 'Clark, I only have what I stand up in! Everything else has gone floating off to London Airport.'

'Never mind, I'll take you round all the shops in Tokyo tomorrow and buy you the moon.' He kissed the tip of her nose. 'And a smaller size ring—one suitable for the third finger of your left hand.'

'Oh, Clark . . . Are you sure? I mean . . . I only discovered a minute ago . . .'

'I knew the minute I saw you,' he replied at once.

'You *did*? But why didn't you say anything?'

He coloured again, this time painfully. 'Oh well . . . you know . . . I'm no good with words. And besides . . . well, I'm pretty mundane and you seemed to want something more romantic. And . . . and . . .'

'Oh, darling!' She put an end to his shamefaced explanation by seizing him by the shoulders and kissing him hard. 'You're crazy,' she said. 'You just don't realize how wonderful you are.'

'Right,' he said, 'while I'm on a winning streak like that, will you marry me? I can tie up various loose ends here in a day or two, then we can fly to England so I can meet your folks. I take it even a romantic like you will agree to let your mother and father take a look at their prospective son-in-law?'

'I don't see why not. I want to show you off.'

'And then we'll go to Sydney. I've got a widowed mother and two kid sisters. You'll like them.'

'Yes.'

He looked at her with mock severity. 'You're not paying attention. I'm trying to arrange our future.'

'I was just thinking,' she said, leaning against him contentedly, 'that the vermilion gateway didn't lead me to the Path of the Gods—it led me to you.' And then she put her arm through his. 'Come along, my darling, we must find Michiko. I want to say thank you to her.'

'For what?' he asked.

She laughed a little. 'Maybe I'll tell you some day,' she said teasingly.

Together they threaded their way through the airport crowd to find their friends. Even the sedate Japanese could tell, simply by looking at them, that these two people were the happiest in the world because they were in love.

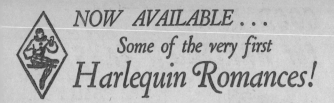

NOW AVAILABLE ...
Some of the very first
Harlequin Romances!

All books are 50c; if ordering less than 6 books, add 10c per book for postage and handling. Use handy order coupon.